BRUISER'S RECKONING
DEVIL'S RIOT MC SOUTHEAST
BOOK SEVEN

E.C. LAND

CONTENTS

Acknowledgments	xi
Playlist	xiii
Trigger Warning	xv
Devil's Riot MC Members	xvii
Chapter 1	1
Chapter 2	10
Chapter 3	19
Chapter 4	28
Chapter 5	36
Chapter 6	44
Chapter 7	55
Chapter 8	62
Chapter 9	69
Chapter 10	75
Chapter 11	85
Chapter 12	91
Chapter 13	101
Chapter 14	111
Chapter 15	117
Chapter 16	125
Chapter 17	135
Chapter 18	146
Chapter 19	154
Chapter 20	160
Chapter 21	169
Chapter 22	177
Chapter 23	186
Chapter 24	195
Chapter 25	205
Epilogue	217

Author's Note	223
Also by E.C. Land	225
Sabotage	233
Lynch's Match	235
Striker's Yield	237
Social Media	239

BRUISER'S RECKONING

This book is a work of fiction. The names, characters, places, and incidents are all products of the author's imagination and are not to be construed as real. Any resemblances to persons, organizations, events, or locales are entirely coincidental.

Bruiser's Reckoning. Copyright © 2024 by E.C. Land. All rights reserved. No part of this book may be used or reproduced in any manner whatsoever without written permission from the author, except in the case of brief quotations used in articles or reviews. For information, contact E.C. Land.

Cover Design by Clarise Tan, CT Cover Creations

Editing by Jackie Ziegler

Formatting by E.C. Land

Proofreading by Rebecca Vazquez

To the readers who love the Devil's Riot MC!

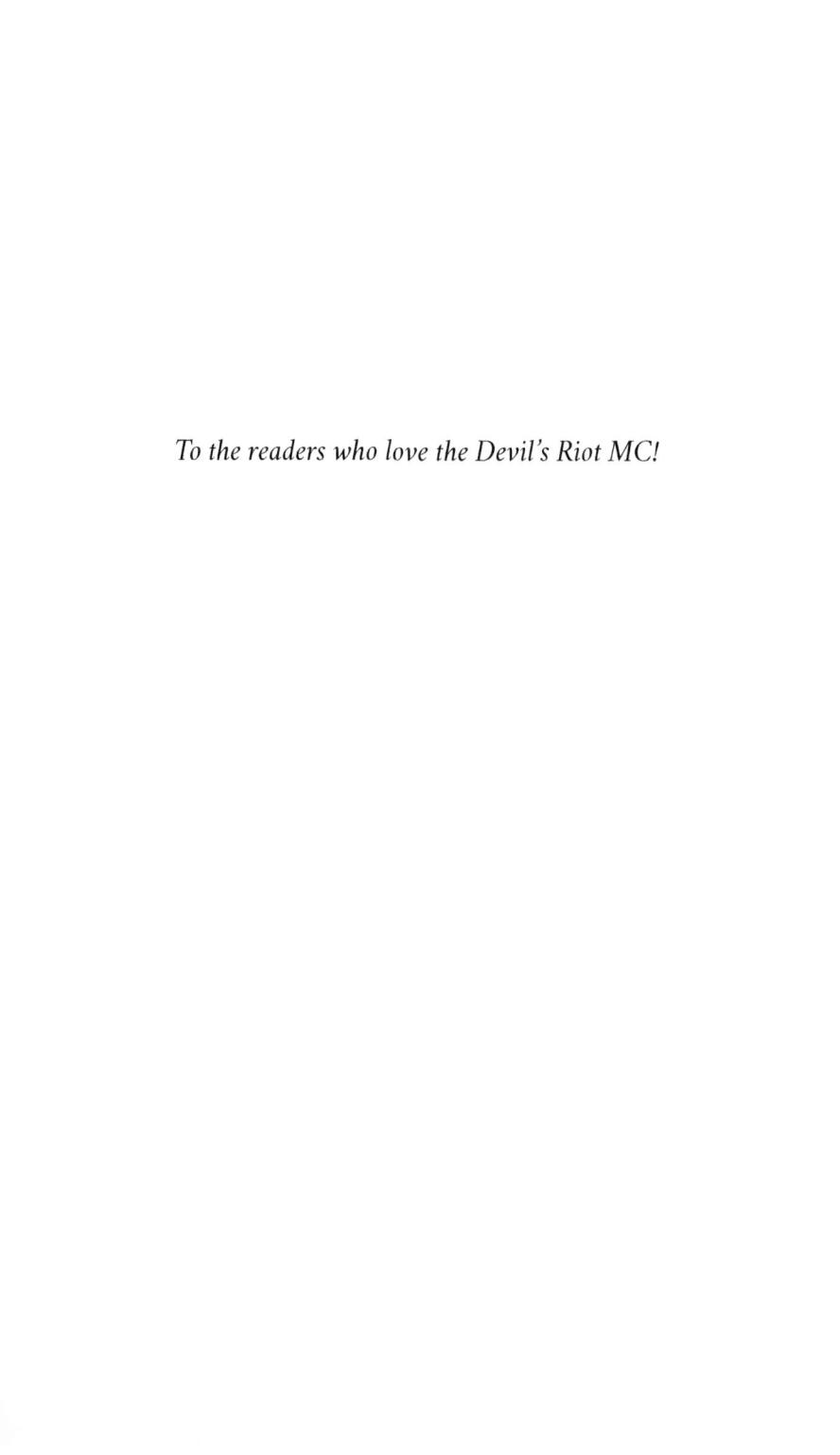

ACKNOWLEDGMENTS

So many people to acknowledge, but first and foremost, my family. They always have my back and support me. My husband and kids are my biggest cheering team, and I couldn't ask for better.

Next, I'd have to shout out to all my readers for sticking with me and enjoying the world I've created.

Then there's my team, everyone who works alongside me to ensure that each book I release is ready to go when the time comes. I couldn't ask for better.

**Check out the music playlist for
Bruiser's Reckoning!**

All Gone – Hueston
You Were Just a Dream – Ava Rose Johnson
Times Like These – Five Finger Death Punch
Breathing – Hueston
Pure Light Of Mind – In Flames
Painkillers – LECADE
Getaway – Eddie And The Getaway, David J
Can't Get Away From Me – Austin Tolliver
Not Strong Enough – Apocalyptica, Brent Smith
War – Phix, Call Me Karizma
Wanna Be Saved – Austin Williams
Saviour 11 – Black Veil Brides
Six Feet Deep – Royale Lynn

TRIGGER WARNING

This content is intended for mature audiences only. It contains material that may be viewed as offensive to some readers, including graphic language, dangerous and sexual situations, murder, rape, and extreme violence.
Proceed with caution. This book does entail several scenes that may very well be a trigger to some.
Also, tissues are a must with other scenes.
Not for the faint at heart.
If you don't like violence and cannot handle certain subjects, then this is not a book you'll want to read.

DEVIL'S RIOT MC MEMBERS
O – OL' LADY C – CHILD

<u>Devil's Riot MC Franklin</u>
Twister – Prez – Izzy – O
Leanna Mercy– C
Horse – VP – Kenny – O
Jason Cole (JC) – C
Kayla – C
Caden – C
Thorn – Sergeant at Arms – Lynsdey – O
William Michael (Bud) – C
Anna-leigh Cleo – C
Rage – Road Captain – Cleo – O
Reagan – C (deceased)
Rosaline – C
Devin – C
Dragon – Medic – Connors – O
Gadget – Tech – Connors – O

Logan – C
Kagan – C
Keegan – C
Hades – Enforcer – Emerson – O
Alec – C
Burner – Treasurer – Ally – O
Lincoln –C
Badger – Member – Jordan – O
Nico – C
K-9 – Member
Red – Member
Striker – Member
Brass – Member – Athena – O
Jesse – C
Mac – Prospect (Deceased)

Devil's Riot MC Originals
Stoney – Prez – Rachel – O
Horse (Scotty) – Stoney's C
Luca – C
Corinne – C
Sebastian – C
Talon – C
Tracker – VP –– Victoria – O
Jamie – C
Jason – C (adopted)
Blaze – Sergeant at Arms –– Raven – O

Matthew – C
Mark – C
Coyote – Road Captain – Tinsley – O
Cody – C
Chase – C
Bear – Former Road Captain –– Momma B – O (deceased)
Rage (Travis) – C
Jane – C (deceased)
Nerd – Tech – Cara – O
Shadow – Enforcer – Luna – O
Daniel – C
Ranger – Medic – Harlow – O
Venom – Secretary – Amaya – O
Whip – Chaplain
Viper – Treasurer
Neo – Member – Harley – O
Cane – Member – Parker – O
Piper – C

Devil's Riot MC Southeast

Hammer – Prez – Avery – O
Tate – C
Malice – VP – Willow – O
Gates – C
Gavin – C
Gemini – C

Axe – Sergeant at Arms – CJ – O
Savage – Road Captain – Honor – O
Gunner – Enforcer – Zennia – O
Delilah – C
Cy – Tech
Bruiser – Treasurer – Gwyneth – O
Dagger – Medic
Rogue – Secretary – Rebel – C
Glock – Member
Ruger – Member
Blade – Member
Colt – Member
Carbine – Member

Devil's Riot MC Tennessee

Blow – Prez – Storm – O
Nines –VP – Meadow – O
Keys – Tech
Lucky – Sergeant at Arms – Chelsea – O
Shiner – Enforcer – Olive – O
Milo – C
Griz – Road Captain
Surge – Treasurer
Scorn – Chaplain
Sniper – Member – Rain – O
Nerd (Nick) – C
Storm – C

Flash ~ Member
Switchblade – Member
Torch ~ Member

Devil's Riot MC Colorado
Grinder – Prez
Blue – VP
Driver – Sergeant at Arms
Flicker – Road Captain
Wrecker – Enforcer
Tic – Tech
Quake ~ Treasurer
Rocky ~ Chaplain
Rex – Member
Player~ Member
Blood ~ Prospect

Devil's Riot MC Mississippi
Viper – Prez – Jade – O
Cyprus – VP – Noelle – O
Kevlar – SAA – Rosemary – O
Aries – Road Captain
Wolf – Enforcer
Black – Treasurer
Vulture – Hacker
Mace – Medic
Sabor ~ Secretary

Falcon – member
Dutch – member
Granite – member
Wrecker – Prospect
Chrome – Prospect

CHAPTER ONE

BRUISER

Following the dipshit who showed up at the clubhouse, my gut's telling me he's up to no good.

I'm not one for bullshit and never have been. It's the way I grew up, and that won't ever change. I learned a long time ago to listen to my gut the way my dad used to tell me—the way my mom did.

Both my parents showed me to be tough as nails. Even now, with my dad gone, my mom is the toughest person I know. She's a hard ass, but still, she has the softest heart. A while back, when she first met Avery's nieces and nephews, she took to them just as my sister Leanna did. My mom is a big help to Leanna with those kids and loves spending time with them.

Between the two women, they've done everything to give them the life they should've had in the first place.

No kid should live the way they'd been living. In a run-down trailer, dirty and hungry. Now, they've got a good life, a woman who cares for them, and a grandmother who adores them. Hell, if my mom were younger, she'd have taken them as her own, I'm sure of it. If Mom could, she'd adopt them all in a heartbeat. Mom had wanted a houseful of kids but only ended up with my older sister and me. During her pregnancy with me, there had been complications that made it so she couldn't have any more. Now, she's got the joy of helping my sister with raising those kids and loves every minute of it.

I refocus, shifting my mind back to task as I watch Simon pull off the road and down a dirty lane. Colt and I pull off to the side of the road. I glance over at him without a word. Simultaneously, we both park our bikes and climb off. There is no reason to announce ourselves. We didn't hide we were following him, but we didn't make it obvious either.

Together, Colt and I take to the woods, staying out of sight and following the path until Simon's car comes into view with him standing outside of it, leaning against the side.

I stop behind one of the giant oaks and lean against it to listen.

"You sure this is a good idea?" Simon asks. "I think this whole thing is bullshit. What's so important with getting in with these assholes?"

Hmm, interesting. I glance at the tree next to me and catch Colt's inquisitive look.

"Because I have plans for them all," the other man states. "They took something of mine, and I want it back."

"And that would be?" Simon prompts.

"None of your concern."

Taking a peek around the tree, I get a good look at the man Simon is speaking with. Something about the older man looks familiar, but I can't put my finger on it.

"I get you think that, Johnathan, but it's my ass on the line here. You want me to do this, you've got to give me something." Simon pushes off his car and rakes his fingers through his hair.

"Watch your tone with me, boy. It's not me who owes money. That would be your family. I could easily exploit your family business to the world, but you help me, those stay a secret, and I don't take Gwyneth as payment."

"You touch my sister, and you'll regret it."

Furrowing my brow, I start connecting dots. This is bullshit, and I'm definitely getting a bad feeling about all this.

"Don't you threaten me, boy," Johnathan snaps. "You do as you're told, and I won't touch sweet, little Gwyneth. Get in with that club. Find a way to separate the women from the men. I want my property back, and while at it, go ahead and get your hands on Honor as well. She's a pretty thing, and both of them would make perfect pets."

Tension flows through my veins, and my hand itches to reach for my gun. To go ahead and pull the trigger, killing both these men. It would keep the headache to come at bay, but I can't, not yet. I need to hear what else is said.

"You promise if I do this Gwyn stays safe?" Simon asks, sounding somewhat timid.

"I give you my word. I'll clear your debt, and so will the others if you succeed in this. But if you can take out the brats as well, I'll throw in a bonus," Johnathan states, chuckling menacingly.

At those words, everything clicks in place, and I know who this fucker is. He's the man who . . . fuck . . . this isn't good.

Another thought pops into my head, and I know we need to talk to Cy. Find this Gwyneth. If we do that, then we'll be able to keep control of dipshit Simon since he seems to have a soft spot for her.

Glancing at Colt, I jerk my chin and start heading in the direction we came from. It's time to get back to the clubhouse, fill the others in, and plan because there's a shitstorm coming, and it's not the one that involves Avery's siblings. Those idiots are being dealt with come tomorrow. This storm has to do with a war that's been stalled. Now, it's happening, and I've got to warn my brothers.

Then I'm going to find this Gwyneth.

"What did you find out?" Hammer demands the moment Colt and I get back to the clubhouse.

After hearing the conversation between Simon and Johnathan, I'm more than ready to get my hands on the woman who seems to be the answer to keeping Simon in check. By getting this Gwyneth chick, we can draw the weasel in and find out exactly what Johnathan wants.

On the way here, I rolled it over in my head. Malice is going to lose his mind when he finds out who's behind this. With everything else going on between the cartel's bullshit and Avery's siblings, along with the satanic group called The Delivers, it became less priority. Something none of us should have allowed to happen.

We all know my VP's family is fucked and crazy. His uncle mostly. A while back, he'd used a clubwhore to attempt to kill not just his woman but their triplets. It was fucked-up all that happened, but I remember Bambi saying the name and her brother, Mario, saying he's the man who was supposed to be purchasing Willow.

Fuck.

Cy hadn't been able to find much on the guy other than a picture when he first looked into the whole thing. That's why I figured out who the guy was when Simon mentioned his name. Then he'd talked about getting what belonged to him. I was able to connect the dots.

"Where's Malice?" I push the question out through gritted teeth. I don't want to be the one who is the bearer of bad news. It usually means the messenger gets a fist to the face.

Hammer looks between Colt and myself, grimaces, and motions for us to follow him to his office. Malice is already in there, sitting in front of Hammer's desk, looking over some papers.

"Close the door behind you," Hammer orders and moves around his desk to take a seat while Malice looks over his shoulder in our direction.

Colt closes the door and comes to stand next to me.

"Now, what did you find out," Hammer grinds out.

"Simon was meeting with a man named

Johnathan." I pause long enough to meet Malice's narrowed gaze. "I got a look at him and it's the guy who supposedly was buying Willow."

"Motherfucker," Malice snarls, coming out of his seat and starts pacing the room. "You're sure? It was him?"

Nodding, Colt and I go over all that we witnessed, including the threat made against Simon's sister and how that's what's being held over the man. It's because of the girl he's following directions to protect her. "If we get our hands on this Gwyneth chick, we can pull Simon in and make him talk."

"I agree," Colt adds. "He didn't seem to care as much about the debt or his parents as he did about his sister. She's important to him."

"Get Cy to find her and bring her ass in," Hammer commands. "If you're right, then we can use her to bring the bastard out of hiding once and for all."

"I'd suggest the women be put on lockdown," I advise, thinking about how he'd wanted Simon to separate the women from the men. If the women are on lockdown, they can't come to harm.

"Agreed," Hammer grunts. "I'll be sending a notice out, but I also want to keep this quiet the best we can. No need to worry any of them if we don't have to."

I give a curt nod, turn, and leave the office. I need to search for Cy, then I've got to get to my mom's for dinner. She's got a rule that she's had since I first moved out when I was eighteen and prospecting for the club. Every week, I'm at her place for dinner. Usually, it's a Sunday or Monday unless something comes up and I have to reschedule for another night. I don't miss dinner with my mom. If I even attempted to, she'd have my ass.

For a woman near her seventies, she can be a hard ass. It's the way she raised my sister and me both.

Leanna is older than me by six years, married a man who died overseas, and never remarried. Leanna buried herself in work and helped our mom out, along with driving me insane. The two of them are known to try and meddle in my life. Leanna seems to think I need a woman so I'll settle down.

I'm good without the headache that comes with a woman.

A couple years ago, Leanna had been at the clubhouse helping out with a few things when we'd gotten back to the clubhouse with Avery's nieces and nephews we'd taken out of a bad situation. Those kids immediately became my sister's world. Even now, she loves them like they were her own.

The nights that I'm at my mom's for dinner, and they're all there, it's always hilarious, and I'm happy for them all.

Still, it doesn't stop their attempts to get me to settle down.

With a slight shake of my head, I push thoughts of dinner aside and focus again on the task at hand. This Gwyneth chick is a priority. Hopefully, we can get this taken care of quick fast and in a hurry. The last thing we need is more drama around the clubhouse than we've already got going on.

CHAPTER TWO

GWYNETH

"I'm so ready to be done with this shift." I'm not one for complaining, but the past twenty-four hours have been the worst shift I've had in a while.

"It's the damn full moon," Angie, one of my two partners, remarks with a laugh.

"I think having to deal with the call with the poison ivy on that guy's junk was the last straw," Mick grumbles with a shudder. "You two didn't have to deal with it. I did."

I give Angie a look while rolling my eyes. Mick can be a bit dramatic when he wants to be. We all can—it comes with the job. If we didn't, we'd end up letting the job get to us, and in this field, as a paramedic, as well as any first responder job, it can take a toll if you let it.

"Well, one of us could have dealt with it, but you simply drew the short straw on that one." I snicker, completely bullshitting with Mick, and he knows it.

The three of us aren't just partners, we're all good friends. The best.

Growing up, I didn't really have friends. Not the kind like Mick and Angie are. The girls that stuck around me were snotty and complete and utter bitches. Total socialites who thought their shit didn't stink. The first chance I had at getting out of that world, I took it. At eighteen, I signed up to take the courses I needed. It wasn't easy 'cause when I did it, I didn't have a dime to my name.

The fire captain for the house I now work in realized this when he caught me sleeping in the car. Not the one my parents gave me, but a beater I'd bought using the little bit of money I did have that didn't go to paying for schooling. Captain Grady pulled me in and demanded to know, in his words, 'What the hell is the matter with me'. I hadn't told anyone exactly who I was before that day. When I told him, he took me home with him and introduced me to his wife and daughter, who I already knew . . . Angie.

That was the day Angie and I became best friends. The two of us have been inseparable ever since.

Neither of us are firefighters, but we're paramedics. It's what I wanted to be when I grew up, and I made it happen. It was the same for Angie. She hadn't wanted to follow her dad's footsteps, not totally. The one who did that was her brother, Ross.

Ross is older than both of us and carries the LT rank along with the privilege of being second in command. I'm personally happy for him. Since I've known him, he's become like a brother to me.

Granted, no one can replace my brother Simon. He's the only one from all that pain in my ass family that I still have anything to do with. Two years older than me, Simon and I were always close, but he's all about that world, whereas I much prefer my own. Still, we take time to have lunch together when my schedule allows for it.

I keep a pretty busy schedule, so it's not as often as I would like to see him. Between work and everything else I do, it doesn't leave me a lot of time. I'm the type of person I need to stay busy. So, when I'm not working, I'm found at the gym training and doing self-defense courses for women who don't know how to protect themselves. Captain Grady and Ross both thought it was a good idea for me to learn to defend myself, and it's surely come in handy.

In this job, there's been plenty of times we've responded to a scene dealing with drunks or junkies.

It's one of the reasons Mick, Angie, and I make a great team. Where one isn't strong, the other steps in.

"What are your plans?" I ask both of them while we restock the bus for the next shift to come in.

"I'm going to find a way to erase memories of poison ivy dick from my mind." Mick snorts.

"You know you love it." Angie laughs.

"Not on your life." Mick gives a shake of his head. "No, I'm going to give Daisy a call and see if she wants to warm my bed while I'm off," he says, wagging his brows.

"I don't know why the two of you don't just make it official." The two of them have been on and off ever since I've met them. No matter how many times we tell them to get together officially, they refuse. I guess it's whatever floats your boat.

"You know how it is." Mick shrugs and cocks a brow. "What about you two? You going to finally do something other than work at the gym?"

I give a shrug of my own. "I'm supposed to meet Simon for lunch tomorrow, but I'm thinking about canceling. I need sleep and to get a few other things done." I hate to do it to him, but I've learned, I need to always put myself along with what I need to do first. Simon gets this and doesn't mind.

"Gwenny, you shouldn't cancel," Angie retorts,

giving me that look. "You haven't seen Simon in a bit and should see him."

"I know." I nod with a sigh. I really should see him. I miss my brother. It's been a month since I last saw him. I mean, I've talked to him on the phone, texted him and whatnot, but we both had to keep rescheduling. From the last few times I've talked to him on the phone, I've got the feeling something's up with him, but what that is, I don't know. "I guess I'll keep the lunch with Simon, then I'll get to the gym. Tell Rico I'll be in afterward."

"You know Rico would be fine if you actually took a day off," Angie remarks and gives me a sly grin. "I could always cover for you."

I give her a roll of my eyes. "I'm sure you would." She's got a thing for Rico, but he's a player. He's not one to settle, and as he explained to me, he knows the type of women who are down for what he wants and those who are the type to settle.

The three of us finish out our shift and get our shit out of the bunks before heading out. I'm ready to get home to my little apartment and crash in the middle of my king-size bed.

"What's going on with you, Simon?" I ask, taking in the disheveled appearance of my brother. I don't think I've ever seen my brother not look unclothed. He's always had his hair neatly in place, shirt tucked in without a wrinkle in sight. Normally, he wears a collared shirt, but today, his hair is all over the place, and his shirt is just a simple blue T-shirt. "Something's wrong. I know it is, so you might as well tell me."

Simon lets out a heavy breath, shakes his head, and leans back in the chair across from me, his eyes not meeting mine. "Everything's going to shit, Gwenny," he answers. "Complete and total shit."

"What do you mean?" Bracing my elbows on the table and giving him my full attention.

"I don't want to draw you into it," Simon says, glancing around and leaning forward to get closer. "I'd never do that to you. Not if I could keep it from touching you, but I don't think I'll be able to this time."

"Keep what from touching me. What is it you're keeping from me?"

"The family is in debt, majorly in debt." He surprises me with his answer. "Because of that, I had to make a choice. Either do what was asked of me or allow the parents to take the easy way out of it. I couldn't allow this, Gwenny, and because of that, I'm sure I've made things a hell of a lot worse."

"You're gonna have to explain this a bit better for

me to understand." Furrowing my brow, I try to figure out what he's talking about. "You need to talk to me, Simon. What's going on?" He's not making sense to me.

"I've done my best to protect you. To make sure you were never affected by the bullshit our parents have created for us all." He goes on to explain the massive debt the parental units have created and how it's affecting the family. "The worst of it all is the man they made the deal with is this guy, he'd pay off their debt, and they'll pay him back with interest. They haven't paid him back, and he's asking . . ." Simon grimaces. "I've got to get him what he wants or he's demanding you as payment."

I fall back in my seat, completely and totally flabbergasted by this new information. It shouldn't surprise me that our parents would do this and be okay with it. They're both materialistic and don't worry about anything else unless it's the next big thing. The newest out there. Sometimes, I wonder how I'm even related to them.

"What is it he wants you to get back for him?" I utter the question, feeling it weighing down on me.

"It's not something I can simply just go and get. He . . . damnit, Gweeny, it's a woman he wants back. This shit is deep, and he doesn't just want her. Now, he wants another woman as well."

Oh shit, this is not a good thing. Not even the slightest. I surely wasn't expecting this bomb to be dropped on me. "Why does this man want those women?"

"I don't know his reasons. Only that if I don't do what he asks, he's coming after you." Tears swell in Simon's gaze, and I can see that this has been hard on him.

"Have you tried to do what he asks?" I hope to God he hasn't. More than that, I'm hoping he went to the cops about it.

Simon clears his head and gives me that sheepish look he gets when he's guilty.

"Tell me you didn't," I mutter, chastising.

"I was trying to protect you, and Dad was ready to sign you over. I couldn't let him do that to you," Simon says hastily.

"Right." I nod and brush my hair out of my face. "Who was it and where? Whoever it is, they need to know what's going on."

I watch as Simon's face pales further, and he looks ready to puke as he answers me. "Both women belong to members of the Devil's Riot MC."

Great. Perfect.

Just what I needed to hear.

Sighing heavily, I get out of my seat. "Come on," I tell my brother and start toward the exit. Neither of us is going to be eating lunch. Not until we get this matter handled first.

"Where're we going?" Simon asks, rushing to keep up with me.

"To get this situation sorted."

"You can't just go and speak to this guy. It's not safe."

"Oh, we're not going to the man our family owes a debt to," I quip. "We're going to the Devil's Riot MC, and you're going to talk to them. This issue doesn't just involve us, it involves them." Plus, I have too much respect for those guys. Well, more like Avery and the other women who work at Rise-N-Shine Coffee. It's the only place in town to get a cup of coffee that isn't not only high priced but damn good. Because of my respect for them, I'm going to them and hope like hell they won't kill my brother in the process.

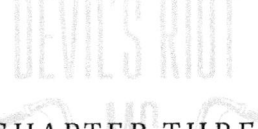

CHAPTER THREE

BRUISER

"Brother, you're gonna want to get out here," Colt shouts from the other side of my door after banging on it, waking me up.

Last night had been one hell of a night, and I needed some sleep. Thank fuck the clubwhores, also known as slobber crawlers, knew the score and got out of my bed when I told them to. I might fuck 'em in a bed, but they sure as fuck don't sleep here when I'm done. No damn way am I stupid enough to let them do so. They'll start getting the idea I want them there. That would be a big nope on the subject.

Throwing the blankets off my naked ass, I get up, snatch a pair of jeans from the floor and pull them on as Colt bangs on the door once again. Colt's damn lucky I didn't wake up with a hangover. Otherwise, I might end up knocking his ass out for waking me up.

I stalk over to the door, yank it open, and demand, "What the fuck is so damn important?"

Colt lowers his arm and shakes his head. "You're not going to believe this shit. Hurry up and get to the main room." He doesn't wait about for me to ask further questions. Instead, he pivots and all but runs.

Throwing my door closed once again, I move to my dresser and grab a shirt from the top. I need to seriously put my clothes away but haven't had time. I make quick work of getting dressed and head out of my room, making sure to lock it behind me.

I'm hoping I've got time to get a cup of coffee before finding out what the fuck has Colt coming to get me. Unfortunately for me, it's not the case. The moment I step into the main room, I'm met with the shocking sight of that fucker Simon standing just behind a woman who's sitting and talking with Avery and the other women.

What the fuck is going on here?

With a quick shake of my head, I move toward where my Prez and VP are standing near the bar, eyes focused entirely on the women. "Why is he here, and who's the woman?"

"The woman is his sister, Gwyneth, and is a frequent flyer at the coffee shop," Hammer grumbles.

"Avery demanded a moment with her before we barged into the damn questioning."

"Of course, you didn't say no." I grunt and motion to the prospect for coffee.

"Avery said she's a first responder. She's a good person," Hammer remarks as I'm handed the mug.

"Well, do we want to break up the party and find out what the hell is going on here?" I know I sure as fuck do. We were supposed to be meeting for church this afternoon to discuss what Cy found and get a plan together to find this Gwyneth person. Now, she's here, and I'm wondering if she's in on it all alongside her brother.

I wouldn't put it past some rich bitch to try it to save herself.

"Let's do it. I've given them plenty of time," Hammer responds, kicking away from the bar.

I follow him and Malice to the table, my eyes pinned on the woman as she lifts her face, and I get my first full glimpse at her face. Beautiful. Makeup, if she has any, on light and natural looking. Her eyes are a greenish blue, and with her hair in one of those messy buns I see the others doing with theirs. Unlike her brother, she's decked out in jeans and a T-shirt. The closer I get to it, I'm able to read 'Primal Fit'. I recognized the name, though I hadn't been in there before. I knew it was owned by a guy named Rico, who also taught self-defense to those who wanted it.

The woman stands and steps around the table, holding her hand out.

"Sorry about that," she starts and nods toward Avery and the others. "I should have told them I needed to speak with you first, but I know your wife and the others," she says and clears her throat. "I'm Gwyneth Kent."

"Know exactly who you are," Hammer grunts, but still shakes Gwyneth's hand. "You wanna explain to me why the fuck you and your fuckface of a brother are in my clubhouse?"

"Hammer," Avery snaps.

"No," Gwyneth says to Avery, giving her a small smile. "It's okay. He has a right to be pissed." Returning her attention to Hammer, she loses that smile. "That's what I'm here for. Seems my family has decided to cause problems not just for you but for me as well. My brother was simply trying to protect me, but he should have gone about it in a completely different way than he did." She pauses for a moment before asking, "Can we sit down rather than stand while I explain everything?"

Hammer nods, and we all take a seat at a table, including Simon, who sits as close as he can to his sister. "All right, now, start talking."

Gwyneth nods and starts talking. She explains what Simon has told her and forces him to explain the rest of it about their family and the debt they're in.

"I was just trying to protect my sister from him," Simon finishes.

"I don't want to cause problems for the club or anyone else, but this man is trying to use my brother to get what he wants. On top of that, he's threatening me to get his way. I'm not about that. I deal with enough bullshit when out on calls. This is the last thing I need. So, I brought Simon here for a couple reasons. One for him to apologize. He knows better than to be an ass. Second, so we can put a stop to this. I, for one, don't want to see anyone hurt because of some asshat or have him come at me."

"How old are you?" Hammer asks, sounding slightly amused, but I've got to admit I want to know how old she is as well. She's got that young look to her but seems to have her head on her shoulders.

"I'm twenty-six. If you need to know more, I'm a paramedic. I work at Station thirty-two here in town. If you need to, contact Captain Grady, he'll verify this as well as the fact I also teach self-defense at Primal Fit and train with Rico. Oh, and I'm an Aries. Anything else?"

Damn, I've got to admit this chick is something

else. Definitely a woman who takes no shit from anyone.

"Yeah, how do we know you're not trying to use this as some ploy of some kind?" Malice asks harshly. "No offense but I know exactly who your family is. Your grandfather is a senator, and if I remember correctly, your father plays golf with mine and my uncle."

Gwyneth stiffens and looks directly at Malice. "You want proof you can trust my word? Call Captain Grady," she states and gives us all a look. "Better yet, I'll give him a call. He can come here himself and confirm for you all."

"I've got Grady's number," Dagger remarks and gives a sly grin. "As soon as she mentioned his name, I sent him a text. He's on his way here and said no one better touch his girl." Turning his phone for us to see it, he shows us the proof the other man indeed said what he said.

"Right, so Grady's on his way here. Now, what?" I mutter, returning my attention back to Gwyneth.

"Now, you all can tell me what I need to know in order to protect my own ass," Gwyneth prompts, leaning back in the chair, arms crossing in front of her, pushing her lovely ample-size tits upward.

"You don't need to handle anything. We've got this

covered. No need to bring some socialite into it," Malice mutters snidely.

I find it amusing when Gwyneth's gaze narrows on my VP. "You might want to refrain from putting me in the same category as those hooty snobs who think their shit don't stink. Unlike them, I know the difference in the smells of roses and peonies, but they still grow in the same dirt animals shit."

There's no stopping myself from snorting at the comment. I've got to admit she's hilariously ballsy, and I got to respect that.

Malice stares at her for a long moment before finally nodding with a grin. "Gotta say, I've never heard it put that way before."

"Gwenny is definitely nothing like those women we grew up with," Simon speaks up, looking at his sister with pride. She gives him a bright smile and jerks her chin in our direction. Something is said in the look, he nods and clears his throat. "I shouldn't have come in the clubhouse as I did or the way I spoke and acted toward Honor. If you'll please forgive me, I'd appreciate it. All I wanted to do was protect my sister."

"Next time, come to us before things escalate out of control." Hammer growls as the doors open, and in steps not just Rick Grady but also his son, Ross Grady. Both men looked furious.

Gwyneth gets to her feet and moves toward the older man, who wraps an arm around her and kisses the top of her head.

"You okay, sweetheart?" he asks as a father would his daughter.

"Yeah," Gwyneth says, stepping away. "Tell me you didn't tell Angie where you were coming."

Ross snorts. "No, we didn't call her. That doesn't mean Mom doesn't know, and she's waiting impatiently at home for an explanation."

"Great, the last thing I need is to worry Mrs. G," Gwyneth mutters.

"Why don't you fill us in on why Dagger is asking me about you and what you're doing here?" Grady demands.

The next fifteen minutes are spent filling the two other men in on the problem at hand. By the end of it, both men look ready to strangle Simon, but Gwyneth saves his ass again.

"Simon's not to blame for this problem. It would be my parents. I'm willing to bet my grandfather doesn't even know about the problems those two have caused. He might be a man of power, but he was never about material things unless it meant something to him politically. He's about the politics." As she's done since she started speaking, she's defending her brother.

I can see these two love each other and would do

whatever they could for the other even if one doesn't think it through what he's doing.

"Gwyneth," Ross speaks up. "You realize this is messed-up, don't you? Some dick wants you as payment if your brother doesn't bring him one of these men's women."

"It's actually my woman he wants," Malice states.

"And Savage's," Simon grumbles. "He wants the women separated from you all."

"He also offered you a bonus if you got rid of the brats, if I'm not mistaken," I remind him with a sneer.

Simon's face pales further, and he nods. "I couldn't do it. It's why I came clean to Gwenny." Straightening in his seat, he lowers his gaze. "I don't want anything to happen to her. I can't do what he wants, and she needs protecting. Some would call me a pussy, and honestly, right now, I'm scared shitless and don't give a damn who knows it, but I'm leaving town to get away from not just Johnathan but also my parents."

Running, yeah, that's what I'd call a pussy move if I knew of any.

Silence descends on the table, and I keep my gaze on Gwyneth, seeing surefire in her eyes. She looks ready to explode on her brother but doesn't.

She's definitely a woman of control, and I can't help wondering what it would take to break through to the woman beneath the ballbuster I can see she is.

CHAPTER FOUR

GWYNETH

Keeping my gaze from constantly wandering and sticking to the most gorgeous man I've ever seen in my life is a heck of a feat.

I saw him when he first came into the room. He has to be at least six-foot-four. He's a freaking giant. One I would love nothing more than to climb and see if the package hidden from view is anything like what I'm imagining. I also wouldn't mind checking out that tattoo that runs the full length of his right arm. I don't have any myself, but I am totally one of those women who gravitate to tattooed men. To top it off and make him the whole package is that beard. Trimmed close, not too short but not too long. It looks amazing with the way his hair looks with that just rolled out of bed appeal to it.

"Look, I know you want to run, but that ain't what I would recommend," Hammer says, drawing me from the thoughts I shouldn't be having. I shouldn't be thinking of the giant sitting across from me.

I shouldn't think of any of these guys, no matter how sexy they are. However, the giant has got them all beat, in my opinion. I swear if Angie were here, she'd be all over him. Or maybe the one who knows Grady. That guy, no, he's got that look about him that would appeal to my best friend.

"What do you suggest I do then?" Simon asks, looking at me. "I can't stick around here. I don't want to risk him drawing me in further than he already has."

I get what my brother is saying. His coming here was a risk. One that needed to be taken. "We'll figure it out, Simon. I promise, but Hammer's right, you running isn't the answer."

"I want to know where to find the bastard because I'm not liking this threat against one of my girls," Grady retorts, talking about me. Ever since I confided in him and he, along with the rest of his family, took me in, I've been one of his girls. No matter the fact, neither Angie nor I live under his roof anymore. Ross doesn't even live there. It's just him and Mrs. G.

"We'll handle that. We know who we're looking for. We'll put a man on you until this is over."

"Ugh, I don't think so," I clip out, stopping Hammer from speaking further. "I don't need a man protecting me. Just tell me who the hell I'm watching out for."

"Gwyneth," Ross mutters.

"Don't even." I cast him a warning look. "You, of all people, know I can handle my own."

"Yeah, I know that. This is some serious shit. You can't do your job and watch your back at the same time," Ross argues.

"Don't tell me I can't watch my back on the job," I snap back. "Mick, Angie, and I always are watching when we're working."

"Enough you two," Grady states sternly, looks at me, and points. "I know you're good and watching out for yourself, sweetheart, but your focus needs to be on the job rather than watching your back. If you won't let someone do that, I'll have you benched, and you know I'll do it."

I open my mouth to protest, only to clamp it shut. He would definitely do it, and I can't let him. It's the only reason I give in with a huff. "Fine. Who gets to be the lucky winner to follow me around? Whoever it is better understand now, I'm not some damsel in distress that needs a white knight, and they better stay out of my damn way."

Hammer snorts and shakes his head. "We can all see that, darlin'. Since you're in the medical field, I'll get Bruiser and Dagger on you."

"Dagger can work on the bus with them," Grady states. "He's got the training and just recertified his credentials. He'd fit in with those in Station thirty-two without question. Bruiser, you'd have to stay in the background."

"I'm not staying in the background for shit," the giant states, speaking up before I can protest to any of this. I don't need another person on my team. "Where she goes, I'll go. Including on calls."

No fringing way is this happening.

"We'll rotate shifts," Dagger mutters his suggestion. "We just need to schedule for the time being. We don't want people knowing what's going on. To keep that from happening, we gotta work this out."

"Agreed." Hammer nods.

Grady and Ross both give my schedule to the men sitting around the table, and they come up with a plan, the whole time not giving me a chance to get a word in edge wise.

Five minutes later, Bruiser stands, eyes on me. "Dagger and I will both be staying with you at your place. Don't argue it 'cause you won't win. As of now, you don't go anywhere unless one of us or both are with you. If and when shit goes down, you won't argue with either of us. You'll do what we tell you." He pauses for the briefest moment. "Also, you fight Dagger or me on any decisions made for your safety, you'll answer to me, am I understood?"

Anger like I've never felt before rushes through my veins, but also something else. I don't know what it is, however, it has the flesh between my legs dampening my panties. This is not something I expected. Narrowing my gaze, I slowly get to my feet, brace my hands on the table and lean forward. As I do so, I don't miss the muttering curses from any of the three men sitting on my side of the table. My focus is on the man in front of me. "The last person who tried to dictate my life, got his ass handed to him. You try it, and no matter how much of a giant your sexy ass is, I'll hand you your balls. Don't think you can tell me what to do. If and when shit goes down, long as you keep me in the loop, then we're all good. But so help me, you act like you can demand me doing a damn thing, you're mistaken. Now, am I understood?"

"Oh shit," one of the MC members mutters.

"Damn, I didn't want to like her," Malice grumbles and Hammer outright laughs.

Bruiser leans in, a grin sliding into place on his perfect kissable lips. "Yeah, Princess, I understand perfectly."

I'm totally in trouble. I tell myself four hours later.

Earlier, after my standoff with Bruiser, he and Dagger both went to get their bags and whatnot while I finished talking to Simon, decided he was going to go stay with Grady and Mrs. G for the time being. It's not what I would have preferred, but he agreed to it. It was his decision, not mine, to make.

Dagger nor Bruiser took their time getting their stuff together. I'm willing to bet they keep go bags ready for days like this.

The moment we stepped into my apartment, both men checked out the place, going through each room. I just hope they know boundaries and don't go snooping through my drawers—especially my nightstand. The top drawer isn't where I keep my Smith and Wesson 357 Magnum revolver that's tucked away beneath the drawer in a Velcro sleeve. In the drawer is where I keep all my toys I like to use. One particular, my favorite one that is, is a blue dildo that isn't small, but I'm betting it's not as big as Bruiser's um toy.

I don't need any of them to see that or anything else in that drawer. Hell, I'd prefer them to look in the closet and see my gun locker there. Okay, so I have a thing for guns. I have a total of ten. My rifles and shotguns are locked away, but my four handguns are scattered throughout the apartment, and one stays in my car.

Like I told them all at the clubhouse, I can take care of myself. It seems as though they don't think I'm capable of this. Whatever.

I'm not changing my schedule for them. I did, however, call Rico on the way home and tell him that I'd be in tomorrow.

Now, I'm trying to figure out what the hell I'm going to do with my two guests now camped out on my couch.

I haven't eaten today and need to do so soon. In my kitchen, I check the cabinets for something to eat, and there's not enough to make something for me and them. I could easily make something just for myself and leave them to suffer, but Mrs. G would be disappointed in me if she found out. Unlike my own mother, Mrs. G taught me to have manners and always offer a drink or something to eat to guests.

This means I need to not only put in an order with the grocery store but also figure something out for the time being. It also means I'll need to converse with them and find out what they like to drink and eat. Hopefully, they don't have a problem with eating healthy. Not that I'm a health nut, but I do take care of myself.

"I'm putting an order in for groceries, is there

anything particular either of you need?" I ask them, pulling my laptop open as I take a seat at my little four-seater round dinner table. "I'm also going to order dinner, so let me know what you two are in the mood for. I'm down with anything as long as it's not pizza or fast food."

"We'll go to the store and get stuff," Bruiser remarks. "You're not about to pay for stuff for us."

"My house, my groceries." I shrug, not looking up from the computer screen and pull up the site I'm looking for.

A moment later, the laptop is shut, and Bruiser's massive hand is the one shutting it. "Said we'll go to the store. Now, get your ass up and let's go."

Oh hell. The look in his eyes with that order goes straight between my legs, making my damp panties wetter.

How on Earth am I going to survive them being here? Actually, the question should be, how will I survive being around this particular man? I've barely even spoken to him, yet I'm drawn to him in a way I don't understand.

CHAPTER FIVE

BRUISER

Son of a bitch. This woman goes straight to my dick. From the moment she stood and leaned toward me, I've had a hard-on for her, and it hasn't eased in the least.

That mouth of hers is going to get her in trouble. There's no doubt about it. My hand itches for the chance to throw her over my knee and tan her ass a bright red. The very thought of seeing her bare ass up in the air, my hand coming down on it, causes my dick to twitch.

Of course, knowing she's got those toys in her nightstand doesn't take away the images, making the vision worse. Especially that dildo. If I get the chance, and I know I will, I intend to see her using that damn thing on herself. It's not as big as me, but it's a damn good size.

During my search of her place earlier when we got to it, I noticed the gun under the nightstand drawer and the gun locker. I don't know who the hell this woman is, but damn if I don't want to find out. I don't think I've ever met a chick like this one. She's damn ballsy, and I like it. I didn't think that was the type I'd go for, but all I can think of is getting inside her, taking control of that sweet body.

While at the grocery store, she fumed the whole damn time. Dagger stayed out at his bike, parked next to her car. When it came time to pay, she'd been livid, and I grinned because she held back the scream I knew she wanted to release. But fuck me, I couldn't wait to hear it. To make it even better, she didn't appreciate it when we got back to the apartment to find Dagger had already ordered food from the Thai place in town. The food got there at the same time we got back. Perfect timing.

"I don't need you two paying for shit," she snaps, unbagging one of the many bags of groceries.

"Princess, get the fuck over it," I tell her, liking the nickname for her. She's surely not a princess in any way, no matter the fact she came from money. No one can say she's a spoiled brat who cries when she breaks a nail. Bonus to calling her princess, I get to enjoy seeing the way her eyes flash with that annoyance at the name.

"Don't call me Princess," she grumbles and slams a jug of milk on the counter. "And I will not get the hell over a damn thing. I didn't ask you two to be here, but still, you're guests. It's plain rude to ask you to pay for things."

Dagger snorts and shakes his head. "Grady warned me that you were going to have a problem with it. But, babe, you're gonna have to get over it. Neither of us is going to let you pay for shit we're gonna eat or drink." He shrugs and grins. "You might as well get over the snit."

I watch as Gwyneth's nostrils flare, her cheeks brighten, and she visibly clenches her jaw. Damn, even pissed she's hot. It makes me wonder what it would be like to fuck her while she's mad. I'm betting she'd be like a wildfire in the sack.

Oh, this is going to be good, especially when she finds out exactly where I'll be sleeping at night. Dagger's taking the second bedroom, and I'm gonna be in that big ass bed with her. Her apartment sits on the bottom floor. It is easy enough for someone to come in through a window. At night, we'll be making sure the door's secure, but it's the windows that could also easily be accessed.

A guy like Johnathan Bryant isn't going to simply

bust through a door. He's a sneaky bastard. He'll find which room she's in and go straight to where she is to get her. He's not going to take a chance of anyone hearing. He'll come in the dead of night, and windows, no matter the lock on them, they are easy to pop open. Especially the ones she's got.

Gwyneth's not in the worst neighborhood, but she's not in the best, either. It's a well-kept building, just older.

Once the groceries are sorted, the three of us converge on that table with the Thai food. Dagger and I talk about random shit, and try to include Gwyneth, but she stares at us silently while chewing her food.

Only when she's done does she speak while standing. "I'm going to bed. I've got to be at Primal Fit tomorrow morning at six. I have a few sessions I told Rico I'd help in teaching." She doesn't wait for either of us to respond before rushing away, throwing her container away, and heading to her room.

"She's going to be a handful," Dagger remarks quietly.

"Handful doesn't even cover it." I chuckle, bringing my gaze from where I followed her every movement to my brother. "This is about to get interesting when I go in there."

"Shit, brother, she's already pissed." Dagger laughs and leans back in his chair. "After tomorrow, she's back on for a forty-eight-hour shift. Way her schedule is set up is two days on two off. When she's not at the station, she's always at Primal Fit helping there. Grady told me that she doesn't get paid for what she does at Primal."

"Why the hell not?" I ask, curious as to what's going on with that. Why wouldn't she want to be paid for something that is considered a job?

"Don't know. Grady refused to explain when I asked. Said that's her business, and he won't give her any more reasons to be pissed or upset. He definitely considers Gwyneth a daughter. Just as Ross thinks of her as a sister."

It's a damn good thing, 'cause I'd hate to knock the man out. Strange to think such a thing, but I'm coming to think that until I get my taste of her, I'm going to be a prick about anyone coming near her.

"You've got a thing for her," Dagger acknowledges.

"I want my dick inside her, that I won't deny," I grunt and eat the last of my food.

"It's not just that, brother. I saw the way you went toe to toe with her. You like the attitude. I've got to admit I like it myself. If you're not gonna go for it, I sure as hell will."

I shoot a glare in Dagger's direction. "The hell you will. She's mine until I say otherwise."

"You claiming her?" Dagger cocks a brow.

"Fucker." I sneer, knowing I walked right into that one and don't give a fuck. "For the time being, whether she likes it or not, she's going to be mine."

Dagger and I spend a bit more time talking about the security of the apartment and plan for the next day before I get up, grab my bag from by the couch, and head toward Gwyneth's room.

She's got the door closed but thankfully not locked.

Opening the door, I step into the room quietly, eyes on the body lying in the middle of the bed. I silently close the door behind me and move to the closer side of the bed. The opposite side of where her gun is stashed. I keep my movements silent and drop my bag, toe off my boots, and strip off the rest of my clothes, making sure to lay my cut on top of my bag. Once I'm ready, I climb into the bed.

Not once does Gwyneth move. I know she's not asleep, though. She knows I'm in here but doesn't speak or turn. I lay on my back, leaving no room between the two of us, with my size, that doesn't leave much when she's in the middle. I relax next to her, arms up, hands resting on the pillow behind my head as I stare up at the ceiling.

"Do you want to explain what you're doing in my bed?" she finally asks, not moving from her spot next to me.

"Someone comes for you, gotta make sure you're

protected at all times. Including when you're asleep. Consider me your bunkmate," I answer, shifting, rolling, and curling around her. "For someone to get to you, Princess, they'll have to get through me first."

Gwyneth tenses, but I don't miss the way she sucks in a breath. Yeah, I'm affecting her the same way she's doing to me.

"Get some rest, Princess," I murmur right at her ear before nipping it.

"How about you go sleep elsewhere, and I can sleep alone like I prefer to do," she suggests but doesn't move.

I flatten a hand on her stomach, just under the edge of the top she's wearing. My fingers span and brush just under the band of her panties. "I'm good right here. Like I said, if someone's gonna get to you, they've got me to deal with first."

"And you can't do that from the other room?"

"Nope."

"Great," she mumbles.

"What's wrong, Gwyneth? Afraid you'll end up doing other things besides sleeping?" I smirk.

"I'm not afraid of doing anything. I can resist the charm. I can resist your movements. It's called training. I don't need a man to give myself the pleasure I need or desire."

Her mentioning her pleasure and desire causes my

dick to flex against where I'm pressing into the crease of her ass.

"I could easily show you pleasure by yourself is nothing like what it could be with me." Lowering my mouth to the side of her neck, I gently caress the skin there with the tip of my tongue and kiss. "When you're ready to have what we both know you want, I'll be right here, more than happy to comply." I pull away just enough to give her the space I sense she needs, but I don't miss her change in breathing and the relaxing of her body.

Yeah, she feels it just as I do.

CHAPTER SIX

GWYNETH

"You gonna tell me what two members of Devil's Riot MC are doing here with you?" Rico asks, matted hands up while I throw punches at him.

"Nope," I mutter, doing my best to ignore the two men. It's more like ignoring the one who slept in my bed last night. The very same one I woke up before, only to find him palming one of my breasts in one hand, the other cupping me between my legs. My panties were damp yet again.

It took me a while to extract myself from his arms and get up. Once I finally managed to do so, I rushed to get changed before he could wake up. I needed to get the gym, and he wasn't keeping me from doing so. The self-defense classes were my baby, and I loved teaching them. Giving those who need it the confidence to protect themselves gives me great pride.

Bruiser tried arguing with me about driving and, of course, won when he threw me over his shoulder and deposited me into the passenger seat. I'd been too stunned to fight back on this. So, I sat there simmering, thinking of ways to make him pay. I was still tossing ideas around when we got to the gym, where I immediately told Rico we were sparring. He's the only one I partner up with.

The first class isn't until ten, and I have time to get a good session in before needing to prepare.

The first good twenty minutes, Rico kept his mouth shut, didn't say anything, just kept looking in the direction of both Bruiser and Dagger.

"All right, then you want to explain why Bruiser is looking ready to commit murder? My murder, to be exact." Rico keeps his voice low.

"Who the hell knows? Just ignore him." I throw another combination of punches and end it with a roundhouse.

"Gwenny, I know you. I also know them. You're either seeing one of them or something's up. Talk to me," Rico states calmly as he motions for me to take a breather.

"It's nothing, and I'm definitely not seeing either of them," I huff and grab my water bottle from the corner of the ring. "I'm dealing with it, and until then, I unfortunately have those two for bodyguards."

"I wouldn't call having the threat of being kidnapped and sold to human traffickers nothing."

I twist around at the sound of Bruiser's harsh words to find him at the edge of the ring and climbing into it. "What are you doing?" I demand, yet my heart starts racing harder than it already was.

"You wanna say that again?" Rico asks. "I'm not sure I heard you correctly."

"You heard me," Bruiser grunts. "You wanna play it off, so be it, but don't lie about the threat and act like it's not a big deal. It's a massive fuckin' big deal."

"Don't you tell me what's a big deal and what's not," I snap, pointing a finger in Bruiser's chest, jabbing him with it. This might not be the smartest thing to do, but he shouldn't have butted into my conversation with Rico. "You don't get to have a say about it, period. You're just around to make sure I don't get taken by a sick bastard who thinks he can take what he wants." I barely realize I'm screaming until the last word leaves my lips.

Okay, so this situation isn't sitting as well with me as I want others to believe. I mean, who finds out their family is in so much debt, they'd get in bed with a bad guy to handle the situation rather than admitting they need help and getting it? Because of them, my life is being threatened. Mine and several other women. Who can blame me for having a weak moment and losing my shit.

Spinning away from Bruiser, I face off with Rico and motion to him I'm ready to go again. "Let's go."

"Babe, you need to talk about this," Rico mutters, turning his attention from Bruiser to me. His head moving in slow motion.

"No, Rico, I don't. I need to be ready if someone comes at me. So, let's do this, damnit, and drop the subject. I don't have much more time before people start showing up for the class." I huff, ignoring the fact Bruiser is still standing not far from where I am.

After feeling his touch, I don't think I could ever be able to ignore his presence, which is something else I don't understand. What is it about this man that gets to me?

"Why didn't you tell me you were in trouble?" Angie demands, storming into my apartment.

I'd only just gotten out of the shower after attempting to relieve myself of some of the arousal still flowing through my veins. My body is still humming with the need for more which simply pisses me off more. Throughout the day, Bruiser has kept close to me, eyes heated with what I hope is just frustration, but if he's feeling what I am, it's more sexual than anything.

During my last class of the day, I kept sneaking a peek at his crotch and saw what I'd felt last night. That hard shaft he's sporting is nothing to joke about. To make matters worse for me, my mouth was all but watering for a taste of him. I even called him up to use him as a demonstration of how to get away from a man his size. Thankfully, he joined without issue.

Well, not any big ones. Every woman in the class had all but swooned at the sight of him. A few even gave him their numbers. He grinned and even flirted a bit, but I saw him toss the numbers in the trashcan on our way out.

"What's there to know?" I shrug and curl into the corner of my couch, aware of Bruiser and Dagger watching my friend stomp the short distance and collapse next to me.

Dagger had been the one to answer the door, and he was staring at my friend like she had two heads because she completely plowed right past him. Bruiser, on the other hand, had been coming out of the kitchen with a glass in his hand.

"Gwenny, you know that bullshit act doesn't work with me," Angie snaps, kicks off her shoes, and turns to sit cross-legged, facing me. "Now, dish. I want to know what's going on and why you have two hunk-a-licious men in your apartment when we both know you never allow any man except for Mick, Dad, Ross, and your brother in here."

"Seriously, Angie, it's nothing," I try again. I'm tired of everyone wanting to know about something I find entirely humiliating.

"Princess, you best tell your friend the truth," Bruiser states using that damn nickname. A part of me hates it, but another loves it. Every time he calls me that, a shiver races down my spine straight to where I crave the feel of him the most.

I swear if I don't do something about this soon, I'm going to end up in bed with him and not just how we were last night. I don't even know the man. I've barely spoken to him in any other way besides frustrated snaps.

"What's the truth?" Angie cocks a brow, eyes on Bruiser, traveling the length of him. "You might as well tell me since my best friend doesn't seem inclined to tell me, Mr. Panty-Wetter." Her gaze comes back to me, and she grins. "Seriously, tell me you've experienced all that is him."

"Um, no," I grumble and shake my head, hoping to keep me from figuring out my thoughts when it comes to Bruiser.

Bruiser chuckles, and out of the corner of my eye, I

watch him close the distance between us and him. He sits on the arm of my couch, his leg touching me, the hand not holding his drink brushes over my shoulder. "Not yet, she hasn't, but it'll happen," he says directly to me. I know this especially when I twist around in my seat enough to look up and meet his gaze.

"No, it's not," I mutter and decide the best course of action is to ignore him. Focus on Angie and what she's doing here. "So, who told on me anyway?"

"Rico." She grins. "I called looking for you, and he told me. He also asked me if I wanted to go grab a beer."

Oh boy.

"Don't get your hopes up, chickadee. You know he's only being friendly," I warn her.

"Oh, I know. He told me he wanted to talk about doing a CPR course for the teens in the area."

He did? Rico didn't mention any of this to me.

"Why didn't he ask me while I was there?" I blurt out, furrowing my brow.

"Maybe because you have enough on your plate as it is," Angie suggests. "Anyway, tell me exactly what's going on. I know there's more to it."

I release a sigh and fill Angie in on what's going on, including the two bodyguards. There wouldn't be any hiding it from her tomorrow when we're back on shift and Dagger's there going on calls with us.

I don't know exactly how it's going to work with Bruiser, but he definitely isn't going on calls with me.

"Speaking of shifts," Dagger remarks. "It'll just be me, but that doesn't mean Bruiser won't be around."

"I'll definitely be around," Bruiser states. "Also, you should know we've got somewhere to be once you're off shift again."

"We do? Where?" As far as I'm concerned, the only place I have to be is in my bed again, where I can sleep for hours without worrying about a call-out.

"Dinner at my momma's. There's no getting out of it, so don't even try to argue with me on it. She'll lose her shit on me if I don't come. That means your ass is at her table next to me," Bruiser says, leaving no room for argument. Not that I could as it is.

Dinner with his mother? That's something for couples. We're surely not a couple. I don't even think I've ever had dinner with a man's mother before. It's kind of freaking me out.

"Oh, this is going to be interesting," Angie murmurs.

"Why do you say that?" I ask, clearing my throat.

"Because I know you, Gwenny." She laughs, falls over, and lays her head in my lap. "You're totally freaking out on the inside."

I definitely am doing that, but I'm not sure I can handle it without having a full-on freak out.

Thankfully, Dagger changes the subject and asks questions about how we handle things on shift. It's a topic I can handle. Though, I know something's going to have to give soon with Bruiser because he's driving me insane.

Something about him just screams at me to jump his bones and have my wicked way with him.

Prolonging the need to go to bed as long as I can, I stare into the mirror over my bathroom sink. I've moisturized, taken my vitamins, and even gave myself a mani/pedi. My nails have never looked so good.

I feel completely vulnerable right now when I shouldn't. However, I know when I step out of this bathroom, I'm going to have to face Bruiser. Alone. In my room. A room that has a very big bed in it.

A knock comes through the door, and I nearly jump out of my skin.

Geez, get a grip, I snap to myself. *He's only a man. A very large man I want to climb like a tree.*

"What do you want?" I demand, throwing the door open, coming face to bare chest . . . a chest I really want to lick all over.

"You about done hiding out in the bathroom?" he asks, sounding amused.

"I wasn't hiding out," I lie. "I was giving myself a mani/pedi, if you must know."

"You were hiding," Bruiser states.

"Was not." It's all I can do to keep from stomping my foot.

Bruiser doesn't bother with a retort. No, his response is to bend, scoop me up over his shoulder, and carry me over to the bed, where he tosses me, and I bounce in the middle.

"What are you . . ."

I don't get to finish before Bruiser's body comes up and over me, spreading my legs to press into me. A gasp leaves my lips, giving him the perfect opportunity to claim my mouth. Bruiser kisses me deeply, thoroughly.

Oh my. I don't think I've ever been kissed so intensely. Passionate doesn't come close to describing the heat of the moment.

A moan leaves my lips as he grinds his hard denim-clad length against me. The ultra-thin boyshorts do nothing to protect me from the sensations shooting through me like a rocket.

Bruiser wraps his fingers in my hair, holding me in place. I'm his for the taking, and I want him to take everything as long as it ends with him inside me.

Sensations lick at my nerve endings, and I want him to give me more. I need more.

Unfortunately, Bruiser doesn't give me what I need. What he does is break his lips from mine. Breathing heavily, he rolls away.

"Now, let's get some sleep. You've got a shift," he says, pulling the covers up over the both of us.

"What was that?" I blurt, unable to stop the question from slipping past my lips. My body is raging with the need to throw myself over him and take what he denied me. But I refuse to let my body overrule my mind. I know better than to do something so foolhardy.

"That, Princess, is me telling you this is happening."

"Happening?" I cock a brow.

"Yeah, Gwyneth." A shiver rushes down my spine at the way he rasps my name and leans in to brush his lips against mine once again. "You and me. We're happening. Get used to the idea, Princess, 'cause after your shift, we're having dinner at my mom's, then I'm bringing you back here where I'm gonna fuck you until you have to go back to work for the next shift."

Well, okay then.

CHAPTER SEVEN

BRUISER

"How's it going with babysitting duties?" Malice asks, sitting next to me at the bar.

Hammer and he called me in while Dagger was on shift with Gwyneth. I'm hoping they've got news on this Johnathan bastard.

"It's going." I shrug and take the beer I'd asked the prospect to get for me.

I do my best to keep thoughts of Gwyneth out of my head. That kiss from the other day has the power to go straight to my dick.

Yesterday, I spent time at the station watching for anything out of the ordinary. I also saw how in the element Gwyneth is with what she does for a living. I still have a hard time understanding why she refuses to be paid by Rico for the classes at Primal Fit. Witnessing it in person, the way she takes charge and gives the women the confidence they need is a great thing.

"Cy was able to do some more digging into your charge," Malice states, getting my attention.

"What did he find?" There're a few things I'd like to know, and I hope he'll have the answers for me.

"Grab your beer, and we'll take this to Hammer's office. Cy will meet us there and share what he found," Malice says, slapping a hand on my shoulder.

I nod, my gut telling me there's something to it with Gwyneth. Why she's the way she is, is what I want to know. Something in her past had to trigger her need to teach self-defense. I also want to know how she's able to survive only on her paychecks from the EMS department.

Grabbing my beer, I follow him, ignoring the slobber crawler vying for my attention. Since setting eyes on Gwyneth, I don't think any other woman could be as beautiful. For that matter, none of them could get a rise out of my dick the way she can.

The other night, when I kissed her, the way she moved underneath me, the feel of her sweet heat rubbing against me as I grinded against her, I could have easily taken what I wanted from her then and there, but I felt the heat rising inside her. She's as hot for me as I am for her. Still, I didn't take her. I teased her until I couldn't stand not going further and ripped myself away from her arms. I laid next to her and held her after she went to sleep just as I'd done the night before.

It'd pissed me off after that first night. I'd woken horny as ever for her, and she escaped my arms to go workout with another man. I would have much preferred to have worked out her frustrations in a better way, one that would leave us both sated, but I let her go.

Once this shifts over, though, as I told her, her ass is mine. I'll send Dagger away to get a break while I spend her time off deep inside that sweet pussy, I'm dying to taste. I don't think any other would come close to substituting what I know awaits me.

Besides, if I did fuck another bitch while waiting on her, I might as well give up on getting between those legs of hers. She's not the type of woman who would tolerate a man who stepped out on her. For that matter, my own momma and sister would beat my ass.

Nah, I'm good at waiting. It'll be worth it. The way she lights up with just my kiss, it'll be like fireworks when I finally get my dick inside her. She'll burn us both alive.

I shove the thoughts away and step into Hammer's

office, closing the door behind me. "What do we know?" I aim the question in Cy's direction.

"Gwyneth Rose Haney, born to Samuel and Trisha Haney, is nothing like either. Growing up, she made good grades, honor roll. Never one to act out. Always helped where she could," Cy says and goes on to fill us in on her past details up until she turned eighteen and left home. "There's a gap there from about six months before she turned eighteen until she left home."

"You can't find anything?" I ask, furrowing my brow.

"Nada." Cy shakes his head.

"I bet she was sent to what is simply called 'The Spa,'" Malice states. "It's where some families send their children who don't toe the line and do what is expected of them. Mostly, it's the daughters who go. They're sent to learn their place."

"What exactly do they do to teach this lesson?" My gut tells me it's nothing good.

"Some experience electrode therapy. Others are forced into drugs that will control them. A few are focused on learning their place sexually. The whole thing is fucked-up." Malice sneers, curling his lip in disgust. "If I remember correctly, they have another therapy that involves beating to submission."

Fuck.

I'm willing to bet that's the one Gwyneth was

subjected to endure. I won't know without confirmation. "Why don't we give Simon a visit and find out if he knows anything about it."

"I'll send Axe and Gunner to talk to him," Hammer says in a way of agreeing and jerks his chin toward Cy. "What else do you got?"

"Nothing much," Cy answers. "She works her shifts. She is damn good at her job, according to the records I've read. In the past eight years, since she first started her career as an EMT and got her training as a paramedic, she's earned the respect of those who she works with. And the work she does at Primal Fit is volunteer. Assuming she went to this place Malice is talking about, I'm willing to bet money on it that it's the reason she does this, and her treatment had been to beat her to submission. It would make sense as to her reason for teaching women self-defense."

I couldn't agree more, and I intend to find out. My phone pings in my pocket, alerting me to a message. I dig the phone out and look at the screen to find a message from my sister.

Leanna: Hospital now!

"I gotta go." I don't bother messaging my sister back or telling my brothers where I'm going. My only thought is something has happened to my mom or one of the kids.

I hope like hell it's nothing and my sister is over-reacting.

I barely step into the emergency room waiting area when I find my sister sitting alone, tears streaming down her face. I rush to her side. "What happened?" I ask, doing my best to keep my voice calm.

"It's Mom," she cries. "I went over to check on her 'cause she said she wasn't feeling well. I found her collapsed on the kitchen floor."

Pain shoots to my chest. It's like I'd been hit by a sledgehammer.

"Have they said anything?"

"I'm waiting to hear something," she answers, breath hitching.

The doors to the back open, and I look to see Dagger stepping through them, eyes full of sorrow. His face is grim as he approaches the two of us.

No.

"I asked the doctor to let me be the one to tell you," Dagger murmurs softly, clears his throat, and delivers the blow. "She's gone, brother. I'm sorry. It looks to be a heart attack, but we won't know for sure until an autopsy has been completed."

He talks, and it's all I can do to breath. My chest

aches, and I feel my world collapsing around me. My mom is gone. She's gone, and I can't do anything about it.

I wrap my arms around Leanna and hold her tight while staring at nothing and no one as Dagger's words sink in.

What am I going to do without her?

Closing my eyes, I breathe deeply, feeling the walls falling in on me. Losing my dad was hard, but we made it through because we had the glue still connecting us all. My mom? Without her, everything feels like it's slipping, and I don't understand. Why did she have to die?

She's the strongest woman I ever knew.

The feeling of someone watching has me opening my eyes once again to find Gwyneth standing just inside the entrance to the ER, looking at me. It's then I realize she was there. She responded to the call and couldn't do anything to help my mom.

CHAPTER EIGHT

GWYNETH

Standing off to the side, I stare at the man, who I don't know yet why I feel so many things for. Mostly, I feel his pain. The loss of his mother. It's something I felt the minute Dagger told me who she was in the back of the ambulance. Upon arriving at the hospital and doctors calling it, he requested to be the one to inform the family. The doctor agreed, and I realized they knew each other.

It's been two days since the news was broken to Bruiser and his sister. I can still see the look in his eyes when our eyes locked in that emergency room waiting area. The way he'd looked at me, I knew he blamed me. He blamed me for not getting to her in time, for not saving his mother. She was an older woman, and it was a heart attack that took her.

When we'd gotten to her, she had a pulse. It was weak, but there. It was on the way to the hospital she coded, and we couldn't bring her back. I've had people die on me before. I learned quickly not to let it affect me, but this time it was different. I might not have known the woman, but I knew her son.

During the funeral, I kept looking toward Bruiser, seeing the pain in his face. I hadn't seen him since he left the hospital with his sister. Dagger ended up taking me straight home, where two other men waited, then took off. I hadn't seen either of them in the time. I ended up asking Grady for some vacation time, which he gave me. I just needed a few days to get my head right. I also wanted to be able to attend the funeral, to show my respect.

Now, standing graveside, I can't stop looking at Bruiser. I want to say something to him. Anything, but what's there to say? I mean, what could I say? Hey Bruiser, I'm sorry I couldn't do more to save your mom. It was just her time. Yeah, like that would go over well.

The service comes to an end with Bruiser helping his sister up, then him, along with Hammer and Dagger, take a few children and each one of them lays a long red stem rose on top of the casket.

I turn away and look at my two new guards, Colt and Carbine. "I'm heading home. I'm not going to go anywhere else, so if you want to go do whatever it is with the club to pay respect, I won't get in the way of that."

"Our job is to watch you," Carbine states.

Nodding, I glance behind me once again to see Bruiser now looking at me. Those pain-filled eyes cause my heart to ache in ways I never knew it could. But it wasn't just pain I saw. There's anger there as well. No matter how much I want to go to him, I can't because in truth, I blame myself for not saving his mom.

I leave the cemetery and make my way to where my car is parked behind other vehicles. With the amount of people here, it's like a maze while trying to get out of there.

By the time I finally get home, I feel raw on the inside.

I go into my room, close and lock the door. I strip out of my black dress, toe off my heels, dropping them right in the middle of the floor. I cross the room, step into the bathroom, and into my shower. The spray hits me, and a gasping sob leaves my lips as the cold water rains down on me. Even as it warms, there's no stopping the tears.

Never have I ever felt so vulnerable. Not in years.

So many years ago, I swore never to be vulnerable again. To always protect myself. I suppose physically I've done just that. Emotionally, however, I'm a total mess. Bruiser saw to that in only a matter of days.

And where am I now?

Alone. Crying in the shower to hide my tears. The last thing I need is for someone to hear me.

I barely register the warmth of the water. Instead, I allow myself this one moment in time to get out all the tears. Once I'm certain I won't cry anymore, I shut off the water and get out, dry, and dress in nothing more than a pair of sweats and tank top. I don't bother with a bra or panties. I'm not going anywhere, so why bother putting much of anything on?

I brush my hair and leave it wet. No reason to blow dry it.

Sighing heavily, I climb in the middle of my bed and lie down, curling myself around the pillow Bruiser had slept on during the nights he'd been here. It wasn't more than two, but in that time, it made it so now the bed is far too big and lonely.

I need to stop this. Feeling sorry for myself isn't going to do me any good. It definitely won't help me get my head on right. Bruiser's gone. It seems both he and Dagger are done with me. I don't blame them either. Regardless, I need to get myself together once again.

Grady gave me the time I asked for, but I don't think I want it. If I get back to work, I can distract myself from what I can do rather than sulking on what I can't.

So what if Bruiser blames me or that I blame myself? It's nothing I can fix. I need to not think about it and let it go, just as I do everything else.

Early the next morning, I leave the apartment, my two guards behind me. My destination predictable. Primal Fit.

I didn't bother telling Colt or Carbine where I was going. They can figure it out.

There's no traffic to get in my way, and I make it to the gym without delay. I'm not surprised when the bikes park on either side of my car as I get out. I give both men a nod and make my way inside.

Rico lifts his head from whatever he is looking at when I step through the door. "What are you doing here?"

"You got time this morning?" I ask instead of giving an answer.

"Always got time for you, Gwenny," Rico states, pushing himself away from the front counter. "You wanna tell me what's going on?"

"Nope, just want to train." I haven't talked about it, and I don't intend to. Yesterday, I made the choice to put it behind me. I don't want to talk about feelings or anything like that. I prefer to work things out differently and without words.

"You got it, babe."

For the next hour, I work up a sweat with Rico in the ring. Neither of us speaks, and this is exactly what I need. Or so I keep telling myself. Another hour passes before Rico ends up calling it quits to work with a few other clients who come to the gym. Nowhere near ready to leave, I move to the treadmills to run. I do this for five miles at a hard pace. My knees are wobbly when I finish, and there's no way I can do anything else.

Deciding to head home, I tell Rico bye and do just that. Tomorrow I'll go back to work. I'll do my shifts and then go back to the gym for another hard workout. I'll ask Rico to get someone else to fill in for me for the time being. I don't think I can deal with teaching others to protect themselves.

Maybe it's time to look at doing something different altogether.

Get out of the business of saving people's lives and find a job that doesn't involve life or death. I could move away, escape, get away from here and the unseen danger.

For all I know, this whole thing is being blown out of proportion, and this guy who supposedly is a threat to me isn't. It could all be a hoax.

When I get home, I'll tell Colt and Carbine they can go home. I don't need a babysitter any more than I need a man who . . . no, he's not my man. Bruiser isn't anything to me. Just as I'm nothing to him.

CHAPTER NINE

HAMMER

"Yeah?" I answer the call, not bothering to look at the screen, eyes focused on my brother, seeing him getting shit-faced and making what could be his biggest mistake.

"We've got a problem," Colt says, releasing a heavy breath.

"What kind of problem?" I ask, finally looking away from Bruiser to meet Malice's gaze.

"Well, for one, after the funeral, Gwyneth locked herself away in her room, then this morning, we followed her at the ass crack of dawn to the gym where she worked out with Rico for two solid hours, then ran fuckin' five miles. Now, we're back at her place and she's barring us from coming inside the apartment. Said she no longer needs or wants a babysitter," Colt reports. "I'm pretty sure the damn woman hasn't even eaten in days."

"She talk to y'all any about what happened?"

None of this sits well with me. I saw the way she reacted to Bruiser, and I didn't miss my brother's reaction to her. Anyone who witnessed them the day they met couldn't miss it.

"Nope. She hasn't said a word. After the funeral, she tried to tell us we didn't have to stay around at the apartment and could finish paying our respects to Lissa. We told her our job was to watch her. Then I swear to fuck, Prez, I don't think I've ever heard anyone cry the way she did while trying to hide the fact she was crying."

Fuck me.

"Don't leave her apartment," I order. "Me or someone else will be there soon to talk to her and find out why she thinks she doesn't need a sitter."

"Wasn't gonna leave, Prez," Colt states and hangs up.

Pulling the phone from my ear, I toss the damn thing on the table, where it lands with a clatter.

"What's going on?" Malice asks, cocking a brow.

"Seems we've got to talk to Bruiser, find out where his head's at and then go discuss a few things with Gwyneth," I tell him, turning my attention to where

Bruiser's got an arm slung around one of the slobber crawlers. A shot glass in his hands.

He's yet to fuck up, but if he keeps at it, he'll regret fuckin' up something that could be damn good for him.

"What's going on with Gwyneth?" Malice straightens, and I tell him what Colt reported to me. "Bet you she's blaming herself." He nods and grimaces. "I saw her at the funeral, saw the agonizing sorrow in her eyes. There was no missing it."

"Yeah, I saw her there and couldn't agree more," I mutter and get to my feet. This isn't exactly what I want to be doing, but I'm looking out for my brother and what's best for him. A brilliant idea comes to mind, and I know exactly how to handle this situation.

I snag my phone, shove it in my front pocket, and look at Malice. "We're going to bait the hook to get Bruiser to get his head back on straight," I tell him, grinning.

"Oh shit." Malice snorts. "This will be interesting. He's already shit-faced. Someone's gonna have to drive his ass over there."

"Yep." One of the prospects can drive him and stick around to sit on lookout for him 'cause I know my brother will be more than a little busy working his shit out with the woman meant for him. "We'll tell Dagger afterward he's back on duty come tomorrow. Give Bruiser a bit of time with her alone."

"This could go sideways," Malice notes.

"Yeah, if it does, then at least we tried to help our brother." With that said, I cross the main room toward Bruiser. "You good?" I ask him as he shoots yet another shot.

"Yep," he grumbles, and the slobber crawler tucks herself closer to Bruiser's side. I don't remember her name, only thing I know is she's a newer chick who's only been around for a couple weeks.

Looking directly at the woman, I jerk my head slightly. "Get lost."

"But..."

"Don't even," I snap, not about to let her even try and argue with me.

"Go, sweet cheeks, I'll find you later," Bruiser says, slurring his words as he releases her.

"Okay," she says, lifting to brush a kiss to Bruiser's lips before walking off, shaking her ass a little more than needed.

"Whatcha need, Prez?"

"You're fuckin' up, brother." I get right to it.

"Don't know what you're talking about." He shrugs and pours yet another shot.

"Yeah, you do, Bruiser, and you know it. She isn't the one to blame for your mom," I state. "She did her job. Yeah, sure, she was there. It was her call. And she did everything she could. I know what Dagger told you, just as he also was on that call. He witnessed it. Said himself that it hurt her to lose Lissa. That woman didn't even know she was your momma, and yet it still hurt her."

Bruiser shrugs and takes the shot. "What do you expect me to do, Prez? I just buried my mom yesterday."

"I expect you not to wallow. You know damn good and well Lissa would slap you upside the head for doing this. And she'd be the first to tell you not to fuck things up when it comes to Gwyneth," I growl, taking both the bottle and shot glass from him. "Also, so you know how much this is fucking with the woman who could be yours, she's barred Colt and Carbine from her apartment as of today. Spent hours at the gym sparring and running. From what Colt reported, he doesn't think she's eaten. I also know from Grady, she called and asked for vacation time. He gave it to her. Doesn't know how much she'll actually take. Told her to just come in on shift when she was ready to get back to it. If she didn't show, then he'd mark it down as vacation time rather than taking her off shift completely."

Taking a breath, I allow what I said so far to sink in before delivering the final snippet. "If she's not going to allow us to protect her, we can't do anything about it. She doesn't want the protection, she's not an ol' lady, or a part of this club. Means we've got to respect her wishes. Colt and Carbine are still there for the time being. I'm gonna go over and talk to her, but if she denies it then, I've got to pull them."

It's a lie. I wouldn't pull them from her protection, though Bruiser doesn't think about it in his drunken state.

Instead, he narrows his eyes and curls his lip in fury. "The hell she's going to deny protection. She damn well better think again."

And how did I know he was going to say that? He's going to go to his woman. Hopefully, they'll be able to sort their shit, and we can get back to business. We've got a monster on the loose to find still.

CHAPTER TEN

BRUISER

The damn woman actually thinks she can deny protection, she better think a-fucking-gain.

I stagger to my feet a bit drunkenly. Since getting back from the funeral, I've done nothing but drink. I figured I'd get shit-faced and fuck, but last night I wasn't able to do shit. It's what I was going to use Clover for, but Hammer intervened. I don't know if it was a good thing or not.

Either way, it doesn't matter. The slobber crawler wasn't doing anything for me. All I keep picturing is a woman who isn't even here for me to touch. She's somewhere else, barring those who would keep her safe. Gwyneth seriously thinks she can bar my brothers from her place. Oh, she's in for it when I get to her.

Shaking my head, I do what I can to sober just the slightest to get the hell out of here and to Gwyneth's apartment. There's no way I'll be able to drive.

"Prospect, take Bruiser in one of the cages to Gwyneth's place," Hammer orders and slaps me on the back. "Don't fuck up a good thing, brother. Your momma wouldn't want you to."

Those words slice right through me. I intended to introduce them to each other the day after Gwyneth's shift at dinner, but it was too late.

This whole thing is fucking with my head. Losing my mom was the last thing I ever wanted. Granted, I knew a day would come when it would happen, but I didn't think it would be this soon. The doctors she'd been seeing had said she'd been struggling as of late with her blood pressure. They stated there was no stopping the heart attack. That doesn't mean I'm not feeling every bit of it.

One thing Hammer said, though I know deep down, is that my mom would be pissed with me if she saw me right now. Drunk off my ass and blaming a woman who was just doing her job. Hell, three other people had been on that call, including Dagger. I didn't blame one of them. Maybe it's because I thought . . . damnit, I don't know what I thought.

If I hadn't been watching Gwyneth, I could have been there for my mom and been able to spend just one more day with her. Who am I kidding? The woman who raised me would surely kick my ass knowing what was going on in my head right now. She'd be the first person to push me in Gwyneth's direction and tell me if I didn't claim what I wanted then she'd beat me with a baseball bat.

Following the prospect out of the club, I make my way to the cage the other man will drive to get me to my destination. On the way, I need to figure out how exactly I am going to deal with the woman who I'm damn well claiming.

Her putting herself out there without protection is not going to happen. She's not about to put herself in danger when we can protect her.

The moment of truth comes far too quickly when the prospect comes to a stop in front of her apartment building. I look in the direction of her apartment, seeing not one light shining through the windows. She's in there, though, I know it. Hopping out of the passenger seat, I'm lucky not to fall flat on my face. Seeing both Colt and Carbine sitting on their bikes, I give them a chin lift acknowledging them, and head toward the door of the apartment.

I don't bother with knocking. Instead, I reach into my pocket and pull my keys out, finding the one I'm looking for. The one I snagged the first day I was put on her ass.

Unlocking and stepping into the apartment, I'm met by an eerie silence. As quietly as I can, I close the door and lock it. I make my way through the apartment, focused on getting to Gwyneth. I don't bother being quiet when I open her bedroom door. I slam the damn thing open to find her jerking up off the bed, wearing nothing more than a towel wrapped around her.

Fuck me if it ain't a damn good sight. One that has my dick hardening instantly.

"What are you doing here?" she asks, clutching at the towel, keeping it from opening.

"What am I doing here?" I snarl, moving toward her, taking my cut off, and setting it on top of her dresser. "I'm here because your ass isn't barring my brothers from being able to do a job they were given." Toeing off my boots, I strip my shirt at the same time. "The fuck do you think you're doing ignoring their protection?"

"I don't need their protection," she snaps and shoots up off the bed on the other side. "How did you get in here? Wait, you know what. it doesn't matter. You can just go back the way you came."

"You know I'm not about to just leave," I state, taking a nice, long look at her sweet, delectable body.

Gripping the belt, I unbuckle while meeting her gaze once again. "Might as well drop the towel, Princess."

"I think not."

The way she juts out her chin, looking all defiant, goes straight to my dick. She's about to learn one hell of a lesson. One that will surely end with both of us getting something very pleasurable out of it.

"Gwyneth, drop the towel and come here," I order, pulling the belt from around my waist and unbuttoning my jeans.

"You can't be here," she says, clenching the towel tighter. "You need to leave. All of you."

"Baby, they've all left. It's just you and me." Smirking, I close the distance between the two of us. I grip her wrists and drag her hands away from the towel. "Let me see that beautiful body of yours."

Without her holding it closed, the towel drops easily, leaving her in all her glory. I take a step back, pull her with me, and sit on the edge of her bed, bringing her between my thighs. With her tits right in front of me, I flick my tongue across one of her nipples. I give the same treatment to the other. As much as I want to suck both perfect little buds, I have other plans to handle first.

Lifting my gaze to hers, it's all I can do to keep to my plan at the vision I'm faced with.

Before she can so much as protest, I grip her waist,

twist her, clamp my thighs closed, and bend her over my knee.

"What are you . . ."

My hand comes down on her right ass cheek, stalling her question.

"What the hell, Bruiser?" she shouts, jerking in my grip.

"Your punishment," I inform her, soothing the sting away. "You got yourself in trouble, Princess, and now, you're getting punished. I'm thinking a good spanking will ensure you don't question your protection again."

"You're insane," she cries out as I bring my hand down on her other cheek. "You can't do this to me."

"Can't I?" I swat her on the right cheek again, just a tad sharper, causing her body to jerk. Sliding a finger between the crevice of her ass, I stroke my fingers through her juices, already coating her sweet pussy. "I think I can, baby, your pussy is drenched for me."

"No means no," she pants as I bring my hand down.

"Baby, if you'd actually said the word no, then it would mean that, but you haven't. Your body is all but screaming out for my touch," I tell her and dip my fingers back into her pussy. "Your pussy is more than ready to welcome me in."

Toying with her, I take my time rotating between spanking her and teasing her pussy. Proving to her that she can't deny what her body wants. Once I give her the full ten swats to her ass, I twist, maneuver her to her back in the middle of the bed. Spreading her thighs wide, I settle in, my gaze drawn to the glistening sight. Never has a pussy looked so good to me. The perfect dessert.

Mine for the taking.

Mine to relish.

Just simply mine, and I'm going to enjoy every minute of lapping those juices like they're the sweetest nectar of the Gods.

The first swipe of my tongue has her body jolting and a moan passing her lips.

Letting my groan be heard, I take my time toying with her pussy, laving up the juices spilling onto my tongue, and savoring the sweet sounds. I don't think anyone could sound as sweet as she does. Nor taste as good like sweet cream.

Using two fingers, I slide them in and scissor her pussy driving her that much closer to the brink of release with my tongue. The way she clenches and spasms around my fingers is all I need to know she's close. The sounds of her moans are a bonus that I love hearing. Before she can release, however, I draw back, not letting her find that orgasm I sense she is becoming desperate for.

"Bruiser," she pants and arches up off the bed, "please. I need to come."

"Don't worry, Gwyneth, baby, you'll come," I tell her and flick my tongue across the pretty little clit. "I promise you, I'll be making sure you do. First, though, you're gonna agree to do everything you're supposed to do. You're gonna let me and the club protect you."

"I don't need protecting." She thrashes on the bed.

Sucking her little nub, I thrust two fingers hard into her pussy, drawing a gasp from her lips. "You wanna change your mind, Gwyneth?"

"Bruiser." The way she cries out my name pleadingly has me clenching my teeth to keep from going ahead and sinking my dick inside her and fucking her to exhaustion.

"Tell me, Princess. Who protects you? Who do you belong to?" I demand. "Who is it that this body longs for?" Driving my fingers in, feeling her walls convulsing, ready for her to erupt at any moment, I know she'll come for me if I just give a little touch to her clit.

"Bruiser, please. Just give me what I need," she begs.

"Answer me, damnit," I snarl, losing patience with her stubbornness.

"You," she screams, and with that scream, I jerk back. "No."

Lowering my jeans enough to release my dick, I grip her waist, line up with her entrance, and drive inside halfway. Her pussy tightens further, sucking me in. I pull nearly all the way out, only to plunge in deeper.

"Fuckin' tightest, sweetest pussy I've ever had," I growl, thrusting home, holding her hips firmly off the mattress.

"Oh God, Bruiser, fuck me. Please, please fuck me."

"Damn right, Princess, I'm fuckin' you, and I'm going to fuck you harder. Give you what we both need." Pulling out, I draw a whimper from her. I plunge forward, making her scream, and I hiss out my own pleasure.

Needing more, I pound into her, gritting my teeth to keep from coming. I intend to feel her coming multiple times before I do so. Being inside her is unlike anything I ever knew. I don't think one time would ever be enough. For that matter, I'm not sure a million times would be. Something about Gwyneth spoke to me from the first time I saw her. She's my match, and I damn well know it.

I'd nearly fucked it all up before I could ever have the chance to get in here.

Feeling her pussy tighten further, there's no way to hold back the release boiling in my balls. I reach between us and flick my thumb across her clit. The cry that leaves her lips is one of pure, unadulterated pleasure. Her grip on my shaft draws the release straight from the tip. I come as I've never done before. It's an experience I intend to feel every damn chance I get.

CHAPTER ELEVEN

GWYNETH

"I'm sorry about your mom," I utter the words I've no right to even say. It's because of me she didn't make it. I didn't get to her in time. I didn't do enough to save her.

Bruiser's hand stills where he'd been stroking along my bare spine. "She would have liked you." The way his voice breaks, but what he says surprises me.

Lifting my head off his chest, I'm struggling with my emotions. Everything feels like it's closing in on me. "You don't have to say that." I pull away as much as he allows, which isn't much, and ask the one thing I can't wrap my mind around. "Why are you here right now?"

Was it just about the sex? Did he actually mean

what he said to me? Or is it because he blames me and now wants to hurt me?

What we did . . . what we shared . . . it was honestly the best thing I've ever experienced in my life. Hands down. I don't think I've ever come as hard as I did when he was inside me. My body is still humming with the afterglow.

"Told you early. I'll tell you again," he says, shifting, pulling me back down, and adjusting us until he's on his side propped up and I'm lying on my back. "What makes you think you can deny protection you know you need?"

"I'm fine without protection. I don't need your club to watch my back," I inform him. Suddenly a bit nervous at the way his gaze narrows. "And who's to say the threat is real?" I manage to ask.

"Oh, Princess, I assure you that the threat is real. I know for a fact. I followed your brother to the meet he had with Johnathan. Heard it for myself what he said. If your brother didn't do as he was ordered, which he's not, the bastard was coming for you." Tension rolls off Bruiser in waves as his gaze bores into me. "I'm telling you, Gwyneth, this bastard isn't someone you want to trifle with. More than that, he's not someone you want to allow to get his hands on you."

"Why did he want women from your club in the

first place?" This was something that wasn't completely disclosed to me.

"Willow, my VP's ol' lady, was sold years ago. She was still a kid at the time by her mom and stepdad. Long story short, her granddad intervened to protect her. We found this all out when Malice and her first got together," he explains, lets out a breath, and shakes his head. "A lot of shit went down around that time, and though we'd started to look into the fucker, it was put on the back burner while we handled other . . . issues."

"Like what?" The question is out before I fully process what he's saying.

I stare into his eyes for a long moment before he moves, falling back to the mattress once more and pulling me into his side. Only then did he speak once again.

"I can't tell you details, so don't ask that of me, but what I'll tell you is because of one situation, we lost a friend to the club who happens to be the mother to Gunner's daughter. Things went down in the club that none of us could stop, but we damn sure fought against it. The women who my brothers claimed as ol' ladies, they've been through hell. More than that, they've come out the other side of it stronger. They're some of the best people I've ever met."

"I know Avery and Willow. I remember what

happened to Quinn. I was on scene that night," I whisper, remembering the fire that took someone I'd seen as a friend. "I usually go to the coffee shop daily to get my fix. Avery's coffee is top-notch. Nowhere else makes coffee like she does."

"That's 'cause she knows what she's doing." Bruiser smirks. "All of us at the clubhouse are damn spoiled when it comes to the coffee. Hammer made sure she taught them and keeps us in stock of the coffee she buys for the coffee shop."

"That's nice of her." It would be nice to do that at the station, but if we did, it'd be gone as soon as we got it.

"Yeah, Avery looks out for all of us." There's no missing the affection in his tone.

Sliding my fingers up his torso, I bite the inside of my mouth to keep my thoughts to myself. There's so much I want to know, only it's not my place, and I don't deserve it.

"Gwyneth." Bruiser's tone shifts, and he draws me up his body, one arm wrapped around my waist. The fingers of the other tangle in my messy hair. He holds me in place, eyes serious. "I shouldn't have left you alone. I was in a bad spot with just finding out about my mom. Losing her, and I'll be honest, baby, I blamed you." There's no hiding my flinch. He sees it and flattens his palm against the middle of my back. "I shouldn't have done that. It's not your fault."

"I could have done more." Tears blur my vision, and my breath hitches.

"Princess, there was nothing you could have done differently. I know this, just as you do." Pulling me downward until our foreheads touch, he whispers words that I didn't expect to hear from him. "We both need to put it behind us. Hammer told me earlier, before I came here, more or less reminded me that my mom would kick my ass for the way I treated you, and he's right."

"But . . ."

"No buts, Gwyneth," he says, brushing his lips against mine. "Now, here's what's going to happen . . ." Shifting us until I'm straddling him, his cock presses inside me, drawing a gasp from my lips. "We're going to spend the rest of today and tonight fuckin'. I'm also gonna make sure you eat something. You're gonna stop blaming yourself. Accept the club's protection. Dagger's moving back into the other room, we're gonna get back to how it started out, and you're going back to work. You help people, baby, and that's what you need to remember. You can't save them all."

"I know that." I gasp, his cock moving slowly inside me as he rolls his hips. That doesn't mean it doesn't bother me when I lose someone, especially when it's like Lissa. I never knew her, but she's Bruiser's mom. I try not to think of it, though, not with him inside me. His thick shaft hits just the right spot.

Bruiser jerks up, releases my hair, both hands moving to my rear where he palms either side of my ass. "Now, ride me, Princess."

Gripping his shoulders and digging my nails in, I comply. I ride him, rotate my hips, and take him fully inside me with each downward movement. It feels amazing. Utterly blissfully.

In this moment, it's only him and me. The outside world doesn't exist. I love every minute of it. Never do I want it to end. Bruiser allows me to take my time, to ride him as I want. At least for a little while. Then he gets down to business, flips me to my back, and takes me the way I need him to.

Talk about mind-blowing, it's exactly what he does. He blows my mind and leaves me boneless, totally spent.

CHAPTER TWELVE

GWYNETH

"What's your actual name?" I ask, staring across the kitchen the next morning, wearing nothing more than Bruiser's T-shirt while watching him cook breakfast, a cup of coffee in my hands. "I know your parents didn't name you Bruiser. I mean, unless your last name is different from your mom's, I know is Gentry."

"My parents named me Dorian Tyler Gentry," he answers me while flipping bacon but looks over in my direction. "My parents were married for two years before they had my sister, Leanna, she's six years older than me."

"That's a pretty large age gap between the two of you," I remark, thinking of the mere two-year difference between Simon and myself. We're close in age, and though we love each other, it's nothing compared to what I saw at the funeral, the way Bruiser stuck to his sister, comforting her and the children.

"Yeah, parents wanted more, but Mom couldn't have them. They were lucky to get me out of the deal," he states and returns his attention to the bacon.

For a moment, I allow myself to think about the night before. After two rounds in bed of him rocking my world, Bruiser ordered pizza. I'm not one for pizza, I prefer pasta, but eating it in front of the TV. Again, with me in his shirt and him just as he is now in jeans still undone. Also, like then, I keep thinking about how easily it would be to slip those jeans off him and go to my knees. Last night, he didn't give me the chance to get my own taste. He spent it devouring me, and I loved every bit of it. Still, I want my chance to pleasure him as well. Though not while he's dealing with hot bacon grease.

"What are the plans for today?" he asks, pulling me from my thoughts.

"I don't know. I need to get back to work. Which the next shift is tomorrow."

Angie texted me about the shift change, stating that she and Mick are back on shift tomorrow.

"You going to the gym?" Bruiser cocks a brow and plates the delicious-smelling food he'd been cooking.

"No." I don't want to tell him that I'm thinking of taking a break. That I thought about leaving the area.

"Why not?" Setting a plate in front of me, he takes the seat next to me, focusing his full attention on me.

"I just feel like staying home." I shrug, pick up my fork, ready to eat and talk about this.

"I know you haven't been teaching the class, Princess. You've been sparring with Rico and working out to the point of exhaustion."

"Let me guess, my babysitters reported everything little thing I did." I scoff and take a bite of the bacon he cooked just the way I like it without even knowing it's how I eat it.

Bruiser watches me closely. "Colt and Carbine were doing what they were told to do. Their job was to protect you and make sure you were safe, Gwyneth. They couldn't exactly do that when you barred them from your apartment. So, they reported in."

"Exactly what a babysitter is supposed to do." I shrug.

"Princess, you need to get the fuck over your issue about having the club watch over you," he states, narrowing his gaze. "Your safety is important as well as those my brothers claimed as ol' ladies. No one wants to see you taken, beaten, or raped."

I feel the color draining down my face at those words. I don't want or need to think about what could happen to me if this man actually did manage to get his hands on me. "No one is going to do that to me," I murmur tersely, maybe even a bit weakly.

"You're damn right. No one is going to do any of that shit to you," Bruiser proclaims, getting up from his seat. He jerks me from mine and into his arms. "I'm gonna make sure nothing happens to you, Gwyneth. So, brace, Princess, 'cause you're in for a rude awakening if you can deal with not having us protect you. Dagger's back on the rig with you and I'm at your back as well as in your bed."

He doesn't give me a chance to speak further. Instead, I find myself locked to him and his lips on mine. All I can do is wrap my arms around his neck and hold on tight.

"Got to ask you something," Bruiser states hours later.

Lots of hours later.

We spent the majority of the day after breakfast screwing on every surface of my apartment. From the dining table to the kitchen counter, into the living room, on my couch, even the floor. We finally managed to get into my bed, where I rode him to climax.

There wasn't a part of me that Bruiser didn't touch.

Including my rear, though it was only with his fingers touching me there. The girth of his shaft, I know he'll never fit. I'm lucky enough that he can fit inside me, period. He's a massive guy. If he didn't make me wet from just looking at him or didn't have foreplay, there's no way he'd get that monster cock to enter my vajayjay.

Lifting up off his chest, I look up to find him watching me from where he's got his head propped up on my pillows. "What?"

"I meant to talk to you about it earlier, but we got . . . distracted." He smirks. "It's not something I prefer to talk about while we're lying naked, but we gotta talk about it."

"Okay." I shift on the bed, sit upright next to him, and pull the sheet up and over my breasts.

Bruiser adjusts until he's also sitting upright, but rather than talking, he leans forward and grips my hips, pulling me up and over his body until I'm straddling his lap. "Don't ever shield your body from me," he commands, kissing my lips with a simple peck, but it's still enough to cause my toes to curl.

I struggle briefly to try to keep myself from grinding against him. Being in his lap, his thick, monster shaft right there, still hard and ready to go, it doesn't make it easy to concentrate.

"What is it you need to talk to me about?" I finally find my voice and ask.

Bruiser's grip on my waist loosens as he shifts more and sits with his back against the headboard, hands going around me, securing me so there's no way to escape.

"Any time today." If he doesn't start talking, I'm going to end up trying to find a way to get his cock inside me again.

Of course, he has to give me that knowing smirk of his that tells me that he knows exactly what I'm thinking.

"As much as I want to be inside you right now, this is important. So, I'm gonna need for you to focus for me," he states.

"Easier said than done," I grumble with a roll of my eyes.

"Princess, focus," he mutters.

"Yeah, yeah, focus." Sucking in a breath, I brush my hands up his chest and wrap my arms around his neck. "All right, let's hear it," I say, doing my best at being serious.

Bruiser shakes his head slightly as if he didn't know what to do with me. He takes a breath, eyes boring into me. "The Spa." Those two words are enough to cause me to stiffen and attempt to jerk away from him. "I see you know what I'm talking about,

Gwyneth, and I need to know what they did to you."

"I'm not talking about that place with you," I snarl, all thoughts of sex wiped from my mind.

"We're talking about it, Gwyneth, whether you like it or not. I need to know what the fuck they did to you there."

"No, you don't." There's no way in hell I'm about to talk to him about this or anything to do with the subject. "I refuse to talk about this with you. It's none of your business. Period."

"When it comes to you, baby, it's my business," Bruiser remarks a bit harshly and tightens his arms further. "Now, start talking before I put you over my knee and give you a spanking you won't like."

"You wouldn't dare." I gape, eyes wide.

"Oh, I definitely dare. Don't test me on this. You don't start talking, you'll find yourself spanked. Spanked and fucked."

The warning in his tone sends a shiver down my spine. I don't think I want him to fuck me with the way he said that. Then again, this is Bruiser, I'd probably take him however I can.

"Fuck me. Your pussy is drenching me," he growls and grinds himself against me. "We'll get to that, but first, you're gonna answer my damn question. What did they do to you in that place?"

Groaning, I bite my bottom lip, dread threatening

to consume me at the mere thought of the place I prefer to think of as Hell rather than a place to be pampered. "What exactly do you know of the place?" I find myself whispering the question.

"That they have different *treatments*," he states, curling his lip on the last word.

"They do," I agree, nodding, "And during the six months I was there, I went through each and every one of them."

Bruiser's body tenses, and his eyes narrow. "You went through them all?"

"To say I wasn't my mom's ideal daughter. I made good grades in school. Had friends, though they weren't real friends." I drop my gaze from his and take a deep breath. "I left home the first chance I had. I didn't take a single thing except for the clothes on my back and a small backpack with only a few of my things that I cherished."

"Gwyneth, look at me," Bruiser commands. I know it's a command, but he keeps his voice calm and gentle, though his body is stiff and ready to strike at any moment if a threat arises. With it just us in the room, there's nothing of the sort except for the story he seems to want to hear.

Slowly, I lift my gaze back to his. "Those six months, I endured everything my mother ordered for them to do. She said it was for me to learn my place in society. That I need to know how to be a wife to someone of our stature. She claimed that the man who was to become my husband would want someone to know how to please him in every way and never talk back. Thankfully, Simon never had to go through any of that."

"All right, Princess, that's enough. You don't need to say anymore. I just needed to know why you do things that you do," he remarks, leans forward, and presses his forehead to mine.

"I do what I do because I learned no one else is going to protect me. I needed to be able to save myself. Never let another person get a hold of me and put me through the hell like my mother allowed. I can't even blame both parents for it. It was all her. My father didn't even know about it. She told him I was spending six months of school over in France."

I give myself a moment to get ahold of my emotions, and Bruiser doesn't say anything while I do so. Because of this, I take another moment before relaxing into him.

"Swear with all I am, Gwyneth, you'll never go another day without knowing someone's got your back," he says, loosening his arms from around me. He slides one hand up my spine until he's tangling his fingers in my hair, and the other cups my rear. "You can protect yourself, but that doesn't mean *I* won't protect you."

I don't know what to say to those words, so I don't. Instead, I lift my head away from his and show him in other ways what he said means to me.

CHAPTER THIRTEEN

BRUISER

"Brother, are you ready to get out of here?" Dagger asks, coming through the station's doors to where both our bikes are parked.

"Damn right." I'm more than ready to get out of here. I'm ready to have my woman all to myself again. Well, as much to myself as I can get.

For the past two days, I've spent my time following Gwyneth and her team around. I've had enough with the men who work at the station all but eye fucking what's mine. If I have to deal with the bastards ogling her body in that uniform she wears one more minute, I'll kill someone. I didn't even know a uniform of tactical pants and a fitted tee with the EMS logo on the back could be sexy, but damn if seeing her in it hasn't had my dick hard for her. I should have left this part strictly in Dagger's hands rather than following them around. But I told Gwyneth I had her back, and I meant it. She needs to know I'm going to be there to watch out for her. No matter whether she thinks she needs me there or not.

The only saving grace for the men who work around her is that they don't dare fuck around and flirt with her. I'm sure they didn't because not only Dagger and myself were around, but Captain Grady and his son, Ross, would probably kill 'em. The first day she was back on shift, I saw how both men watched over her, checking her pulse, ensuring themselves she was good. I didn't blame them for it either. She's still not exactly a hundred percent. The woman is getting there, though she's hiding something, and it has to do with her working at the gym.

I talked to Colt and Carbine to see how she acted at the gym. They both said exactly what they'd reported to Hammer. I figured when I took her there tomorrow, I'd talk to Rico and see if he's noticed something off about her. He'd know her best other than Angie and Mick, who she works with.

I'll be happy when she finishes the day out, and I can get her ass back in bed and then bury myself deep inside her pussy.

I have plans for the two of us, plans I intend to enjoy. I'm thinking instead of going to her apartment, we'll go to the clubhouse. Stay in my room there. The club's having a party tomorrow night, and I wouldn't mind seeing Gwyneth cut loose and have a bit of fun. I don't have to worry about her and the slobber crawlers. They fuck with her, it's their funeral. I know it. My brothers know it. So do the ol' ladies.

"You takin' her to the clubhouse or apartment?"

"Clubhouse," I answer seeing the look on Dagger's face. One of sweet relief. "What's with the look?"

"After being on shift with those three, I'm ready to do my head in. I need to get away from the headache," Dagger grumbles while straddling his bike. "If I have to hear either of those women, or Mick, for that matter, talk about sex, orgasms, and the best positions to reach ultimate climax. I can't deal with more of it. I don't want to know about Mick and his girl's relationship, how they're off once again. I don't want to hear about Angie's need for sex. Hell, the woman even offered to take me for a spin. No damn way would I touch Grady's daughter." He blows out a frustrated breath and glares at me. "I also don't need to hear about your ugly ass and the spanking you gave Gwyneth." He grimaces.

I throw my head back and burst out laughing. I

can't help it. I don't think I've ever seen my brother this put out about anything.

"What has you laughing?"

I cock my head in Gwyneth's direction and grin at the sight of her. She changed from her uniform into a pair of form-fitting jeans, ankle boots, and a tank top that covers her tits just the right amount not to be inappropriate. The woman is damn lucky she's walking out of that station and to me rather than into it.

Fuck me. She's sex on a stick, and I can't wait to get my mouth on that sweet pussy again.

"Nothing, Princess," I answer, sobering. "You ready to go?"

"Yeah, I'm ready." She makes her way to me, and my dick hardens even further with the way she sways her hips. "What are we doing?"

"Going to the clubhouse," I inform her while straddling my bike and motioning for her to hop on. The other day was the first time she'd been on my bike or any bike. I like the fact no one else has ever given her a ride, and my bike is the only one she ever gets on the back of.

The moment she's got her arms wrapped around my waist, her body firmly pressed against mine, I squeeze the throttle and jerk my chin up toward

Dagger. Time for me to show my woman how to have a good time.

"We've got a problem," Cy says, taking a sip of his beer, sitting next to me, eyes focused on the women dancing in the middle of the room.

Tonight, we've got more than just the slobber crawlers or the ol' ladies here. Every so often, we let hangarounds and some strange in for a party. We haven't done it much lately, and it's all good, it means less to clean up afterward. Granted, that's nothing I handle.

"What's the problem?" I ask, not taking my eyes off my woman as she dances, swaying to the music thumping through the speakers, with a few of the other ol' ladies. I might not have officially claimed her, but damn, if I don't like the idea of her being just that for me. I'll have to get her a property cut like the others have on.

"I've been digging deeper into your woman's background," he remarks.

"And . . ." I promote.

"And I have a feeling that she's not actually Simon's sister, well more like half-sister," he states, getting my full attention.

"The fuck do you mean by that? What have you found?"

Cy twists on his stool, motions to the prospect working behind the bar tonight for two shots, and finally looks directly at me. "From what I've been able to find so far, the only record of her mother giving birth is to Simon. No other records. Nothing on about surrogates or anything else. What I did find was the father had a mistress, and that mistress died shortly after giving birth due to complications. Her father took her in. They had nannies and all that shit."

"You're thinking the mother is behind all of the shit?" I cock a brow and grab one of the two shots the prospect sat on the bar top.

"I'm not sure about that, but she's not Gwyneth's mother," Cy remarks and throws his own shot back. "I looked more into the mistress and found family relations. You won't believe who, though."

"Do I even want to know?" I quip, feeling my good mood slipping away.

"This is the interesting part," he states, leaning closer. "The mistress's name was Gwendolyn Rose."

"So, the father named his daughter after the mistress?" I glance back to the dance floor, checking on my woman, my gut twisting.

"You got it. Gave her a somewhat different name, but the same still. Gwyneth's birth certificate doesn't show that name, though. It's Simon's mother's name on it. They hid this from the world. But I'm thinking you get the father alone, he'll confirm all of this."

"Right." I nod, not liking any of this. "Now that you told me this, what's the actual problem you said we have?"

"The fact is, it wasn't the father who made the deal with Johnathan to get them out of debt. It was the mother, and I was able to hack into phone records along with email. Just this afternoon, she's given her blessing to Johnathan to have Gwyneth, even if that means killing her son to get what he wants as long as he wipes the debt clear. A response came in right before I came to talk to you, Johnathan has responded that he will take this offer."

Shit. Shit. Fucking bullshit.

"Means we need to bring Simon in to protect him. Otherwise, his ass is as good as dead," I snarl. I'm going to have to talk to Gwyneth about this. She's got a right to know, but it's going to suck having to tell her. Then again, it might not be so shocking considering how her mother treated her about the whole ordeal she had to go through for those months at that fucking spa.

"You got it. We've got church tomorrow at noon. I figured this could wait that long, though, I wanted to give you a heads up."

"Appreciate it," I say, nodding. "We need to get someone on Simon tonight."

"Sent a text to both Grady men, and they've got it under control for tonight and will bring Simon here to the clubhouse tomorrow," Cy states and slaps me on the back. "Enjoy tonight with your woman." He gives me that shit-eating grin he's known for and walks away.

Returning my attention to Gwyneth, it's all I can do to keep from going to her, throwing her over my shoulder, and taking her to my room for a different kind of dance.

I'm about ready to do just that when Clover takes the moment to wrap herself around me.

"Hey, baby, I've missed you around here," the seductive note in Clover's voice isn't missed. "You wanna go finish what we'd started the other night?"

"Nope," I tell her and push her off me without hurting her. "And for the record, nothing was gonna happen, so don't go twisting words." I may have been shitfaced and flirting. Hell, I might have let her blow me, but I wouldn't have fucked her. It makes me an ass even to think I'd let her blow me. I'd been fucked in the head with all the shit going on. Between thoughts of my mom and blaming my woman, it was all fucked-up.

"Come on, Bruiser, you know we'd have a good

time," Clover purrs, stroking a finger up and down the front of my shirt.

"You might want to back the hell off," I advise, spotting my woman coming closer.

"Why? Because of that woman you brought with you?" She huffs. "You know she's not going to give you what you need? I've heard about how you like to fuck hard, Bruiser, she's not gonna let you do the dirty with her. And you know it."

"Back off," I warn her one last time as Gwyneth gets to us.

"Is there a reason you have a skank wrapping herself around you?" she asks, looking at me. "If I knew you were bringing me here so you could fuck sloppy, you should have told me—"

"Princess, don't even finish that sentence," I snarl, yanking her to me. One hand cupping her ass, the other going up to tangle in her hair. I dip my head down until we're nose to nose. "The only pussy I want in is yours, baby, and you damn well know it." I don't give her a chance to respond because, in the next instant, I claim her lips with mine, tongue thrusting in her mouth, right there in a room full of people.

At the sound of catcalls and whistles over the loud thumping music, I break the kiss and meet her gaze once again. "Now, you either get back to dancing or you ready to get fucked by your man?"

Rather than answering me with words, Gwyneth does as she always does and goes for what she wants. Jumping in my arms, she wraps her legs around my waist as I grip her hips, her lips coming back to mine.

Now, that's what I'm talking about.

CHAPTER FOURTEEN

GWYNETH

Ignoring the sounds around us, I hold tight and keep on kissing Bruiser. Not only because I want this, I'm making a statement. Not just to the bitch who dared touch him, but to all of them. Bruiser is mine, and I'm not going to let them have what's mine.

Okay, so it seems an idiot thing to do, but Bruiser doesn't seem to mind one bit, me literally jumping him.

Bruiser doesn't pull away or attempt to push me off him. He gave me the choice of going back to having fun with women I see as friends or to have him fuck me. Well, as much fun as I was having with Avery and the others, I'm totally down with having him inside me again. It's all I could do the past two days to keep from finding a closet to drag his ass into to have him take me, to feel his arms around me for just a few moments.

Unfortunately, I'd been professional and didn't do as I wanted. That didn't mean I didn't visualize what I wanted to do to him. Angie and I even talked about the different positions I look forward to trying with him. I'm definitely not a prude who only wants vanilla, and I think I proved that to Bruiser more than once during the day of screwing all over my apartment. He's the one who kept throwing me to my back and plowing into me like a jackhammer. Not that I would ever complain, I loved that he took charge.

The moment we're alone in Bruiser's room, he turns me so my back is against the door and grinds himself against me. A moan slips past my lips, loving what he's doing to me. It feels amazing. My panties are drenched from my need for him.

Bruiser rips his lips from mine and trails kisses along my jaw and my neck, licking and nipping his way downward.

From there, everything escalates. Clothes are ripped off as Bruiser moves us to the bed. Once there, I'm tossed in the middle with him coming over me.

"Two days without being in this sweet body is way too damn long." A shiver rushes down my spine at the intensity of his husky voice. "I'm not waiting a moment longer than I have to."

"Take me, Bruiser. Fuck me like I'm dying for you to do." I arch into his touch, needing to feel his hands all over me, his dick inside me, feel him consuming me the way only he can do so.

"Don't worry, Princess, I'm gonna fuck you." He draws a gasp from my lips when he cups me between my legs and plunges two fingers inside me. "Fuckin' love how wet you get for me. You get like this for anyone else?"

"No," I pant, moving against his fingers, needing them deeper.

"Think I'd get this hard for some other bitch?" he demands, pulling his fingers from inside me only to replace them with his shaft thrusting inside me.

"Oh God," I moan at the sheer intensity of him working inside me.

"Answer me, Gwyneth, do you think I'd get this hard for some other bitch?" He pulls nearly all the way out, only to plunge deeper inside. "Fuck, baby, you're so damn tight, even with your pussy drenched for me, you're clenching me like a damn vice. With the way you clutch at me dick, you think I want anything else?" he demands, stilling fully seated inside me.

"No, Bruiser, I don't think . . ."

"You're damn right you didn't think," he growls,

reaches between us, and strums his thumb over my clit. "The only pussy I want in is this one."

"Bruiser," I cry out, burning need flaming up inside me as he starts moving faster. Harder. More intensely. It's heaven and hell all in one. "Oh God, Bruiser, it's so good."

"Damn right it is," he snarls, jerks my knees up and over his shoulders, and grips my hips, changing the depths of which he takes me. The pleasure becomes nearly too much, yet I hunger for more. So much more.

The orgasm that rushes through me, over me, flares within the pit of my entire being is truly my undoing. Emotions I never knew I could feel wash over me, and I know in this moment in time, my world is forever changed. Bruiser changed it in ways I don't understand. Screaming his name, I cling to him, needing to hold on to something to keep myself grounded.

I thought Bruiser might join me in the throes of release, but he doesn't. Instead, he pulls out, rolls me to my stomach, jerks my lower half up, and thrusts back inside me with enough force to cause my stomach to bow and a scream of unadulterated pleasure to leave my lips.

"That's it, Princess, scream for me. Let me hear how much you love taking my dick," he states and tightens his grip on my hips, driving his shaft deeper . . . harder.

I claw at the sheets beneath me to keep myself from falling over. It's all I can do to keep myself up. When my second release hits, waves of ecstasy thrum through my veins, and I don't recognize the sound of my own voice crying out for him. I'm drowning in a sea of liberation, my mind and body at one with the floodgates open to each and every sensation Bruiser draws out of me.

Bruiser's fingers tighten further, holding me in place as he pummels inside, drilling into me with furious thrusts, roaring my name as he comes, spurting his own release.

Falling face forward into the pillows, it's all I can do to get my breathing under control. Bruiser's much bigger body collapses over me, but he holds himself off me with his arms caging me in on either side of my arms.

"Princess, that was . . . fuck, I don't have words for how good it was." He releases a breath and presses a kiss on my bare shoulder.

"I think you've ruined me for ever having sex any other way," I blurt out. "I don't think I ever want slow vanilla sex ever again."

Bruiser chuckles and pulls out, which causes me to whimper at the loss of him. Rolling to his side, he takes me with him. "Don't worry, baby, when I'm feeling like taking you slow again, you'll love it as much as you love what we just did. Now, rest up, 'cause we're nowhere near done. I've got two days to make up for."

"Is this what you plan on doing every time I get off a shift?" I ask, peeking up at him through my lashes.

"Damn right," he answers, grinning, cupping the back of my head, tangling his fingers in my hair. "Warning you now. Brace, Princess, I got to put up with you at that station, men eye fuckin' you, I'm gonna fuck you however I please when I get you to myself again."

I barely register those words before he's on me again.

I guess we won't be doing any resting up, which I don't mind. Not in the least.

CHAPTER FIFTEEN

GWYNETH

"We've gotta talk about something," Bruiser utters, leaning into my back, lips at my ear.

"About what?" I ask, turning in his arms.

He left me with my friends early to go into a room that they call church. I don't know much about MCs and their politics, but I'm sensing that whatever it is, it's important to the members of the club.

"Let's go to my room. We'll talk about it in there," he says, wrapping an arm around my waist and pulling me firmly into him.

"Um, okay." I lick my lips somewhat nervously. Any conversation that begins with any sort of 'We need to talk' can't be good. Right?

Bruiser guides me through the clubhouse until

we're in his room. He drops his arm away and starts pacing in front of the bed. Hands on his hips, head dipped downward.

"You going to tell me what's going on?" I ask, climbing into the middle of the bed, sitting with my legs crossed, fingers together. "Did something happen? You were fine earlier." Okay, I don't bother hiding the blush I know is tinting my cheeks when I think exactly what he and I did after waking up tangled in each other's arms.

Throughout the night, he'd taken me repeatedly. Always in different positions, but each time ended with him on top and coming deep inside me. It's definitely a good thing that I'm on birth control. We haven't talked about it, but I'm going to have to say something. I mean, I know I'm clean, and I'm pretty sure he wouldn't have sex with me unprotected unless he were clean. I've rarely had sex unless it was by myself with my toys.

Bruiser faces me with a grim look. "I've got something I need to tell you, and you're not gonna like it."

"Unless it's you telling me that you've got some disease and I now have it, I think I can handle it," I state, pulling my legs up and wrapping my arms around them.

"What?" He blinks and stares at me like I've grown

two heads. "You think I'd fuck you without protection and give you some shit?"

"Well, we've never talked about it." I shrug and bite my bottom lip.

"You could have asked if you wanted to know, Princess," he grumbles and goes back to pacing. "I've never fucked a woman other than you without a condom. I've never let a bitch blow me without a condom."

"You haven't even let me do that," I blurt before I can stop the words from coming out.

That stops him in his tracks, and he comes to the end of the bed, leans in, bracing his upper body on the bed with his hands, and gets in my face. "Gwyneth, any other time, I'd pull my dick out and tell you to get on your knees and let me fuck your pretty little mouth."

"That would be interesting," I barely breathe out before I find myself flat on my back and Bruiser hovering over me.

"Woman, if you don't get your mind out of the gutter, I'm going to put you over my knee."

"And that's a bad thing?" Okay, if I don't stop, I'm really going to get myself in trouble.

"Swear to God, Princess, your ass is in trouble," he snarls and jerks away. "You've earned a spanking, baby, be warned, I'm not forgetting about it, but I've got more important shit that we gotta talk about."

"Okay." I pout, sitting back up. "For the record, we don't have to worry about you knocking me up. I'm on the pill."

"I know you are." Smirking, he cocks a brow. "I saw the pills in the drawer next to your toys."

"You did not." I gasp, eyes widening.

"Oh yeah, I did. Don't think I don't intend to use that purple dildo on you, Princess. I want to watch as your pussy sucks it right on in. Maybe I'll fuck your ass while you've got your pussy filled with your toy."

"Oh my God," I breathe, trying not to think of how much the thought turns me on.

"Yeah, baby, brace for what's to come your way," he says, that smirk tilting up into a panty-melting grin. "Now, stop trying to get me to fuck you by looking fuckable and listen, 'cause what I'm gonna tell you is going to be unpleasant."

Licking my lips, I nod. "Okay, shoot. Let me have it." It has to be important, otherwise, he wouldn't be turning down a chance to fuck me silly.

I take in the grim expression on Bruiser's face and the way his body tenses. Not in the way I like either. Yeah, whatever it is, it's not only important but also going to be ugly.

"Go ahead and get it out, Bruiser," I murmur, dreading what he may say.

Bruiser sits back down and takes one of my hands in his. "Cy was doing some digging. Trying to figure shit out."

"Okay . . ." I draw out the word and lick my lips. "Did he find something?"

"Yeah, you can say he found something." He grunts, lips thinning in a grimace. "But I've got to ask you something 'cause it's not sitting right with me. The way you spoke about her and The Spa . . ."

Now, it's my turn to tense. "What about my mom?"

"Did you know that she's not your biological mother?" he asks me, eyes boring into mine.

Sucking in a breath, I nod slowly and answer. "Not because she told me or anything like that. Angie and I did a DNA test to find out ancestry. Simon had told me about the family having done one. I didn't know it until then, but it doesn't surprise me. I've kept it to myself. I mean, regardless of blood relations, she's the woman who raised me."

"Right," he says, his jaw visibly ticking. "You didn't know this beforehand?"

"No."

"Then this may hurt you, what I'm about to tell you," he mutters more to himself than me.

"Whatever it is, just say it, Bruiser. I'm a big girl

and can take it," I snap, getting frustrated by the minute.

Bruiser reaches out, cups the side of my face, and strokes my cheek. "Remember me telling you the other day I've got your back? This is me doing just that. Protecting you. Not dropping a bomb on you that could hurt you more than you've been hurt in the past."

My stomach flutters and tightens. I really like that he'd say something so sweet to me. No one has ever said anything so sweet to me in my life. "I appreciate it, but just rip the Band-Aid and tell me everything."

Nodding, Bruiser continues to stroke my cheek and rips the Band-Aid right off. "Cy found an email between her and Johnathan Bryant, the man who I saw your brother meet. In the email, she pretty much told him to kill your brother, and he could have you."

Whoa.

I didn't see that coming.

She loves Simon, and yet she'd kill him? That doesn't make sense unless her show of affection for Simon was just a mask to the rest of the world.

"What else is there?" I ask, knowing deep down he's not done yet.

A moment passes in silence before he breaks it. "During church, we've all agreed Simon is to be sent to a safe house to keep him out of the line of fire. Unfortunately, though, we can't find where Johnathan is holding himself up. However, we did find out he's associated with a group that calls themselves the Supreme Masters, but we also know the organization was crippled majorly when one of the head honchos was killed. Those are details I won't share. It's not something you need to know."

"Trust me, I don't want to know how somebody was killed." I shudder at the thought. He probably deserved it. I don't know what the Supreme Masters organization is, but the way Bruiser speaks of it, like it leaves a bad taste in his mouth, it has to be bad.

"This bastard is one sick fucker, though. He doesn't want just you. He wants Willow and Honor. I'm willing to put money on it if he could take CJ, Rebel, and Avery, he'd snatch them up too. Make it a full collection," Bruiser mutters, shaking his head.

Full collection.

Why does that sound familiar?

"We need to keep you safe. Keep the other ol' ladies safe."

"I'm not an ol' lady," I blurt, not meaning too.

"Princess." The warning in his voice is the only thing I get before he's over me once again, me going to my back. He cages me in and gets in my face, nose pressing to my nose. "Don't try to argue with me on this, 'cause I'll tell you now, you won't win. When it comes to you and me, you're damn well mine. My woman. My ol' lady. Fuckin' mine."

He slams his mouth to mine, and all other thoughts go out of my mind.

There's no fear for my brother.

No nothing.

Right here in Bruiser's arms, there's no fear that something could happen. That I'll be taken away from my life.

In this moment, same as any time Bruiser is touching me, I'm safe, and nothing else matters.

CHAPTER SIXTEEN

BRUISER

"Someone needs to answer for this."

I glance up from my coffee to find Dagger prowling in the kitchen, looking far more pissed than I've ever seen him.

"What's going on?" Gwyneth asks before I get the chance, plopping down next to me with her cup of coffee.

It's been a week of her going on and off shift, but she'd yet to go back to the gym to teach herself defense class. She hasn't said much about her brother being put into a safe house or the situation in general. Any time I ask her about it, she shrugs and says, 'What could she do besides let me and Dagger keep her safe?'.

Her thinking on it isn't wrong but at the same time, I don't like it.

Gwyneth is a feisty, take-charge, on-top-of-the-world type of person, and for her to not want to be a part of her own safety means something's going on in her head. In the time since I first met her, she's not been one to back down, so I'm finding it a bit hard not to question her about it. I just hadn't pushed the issue yet. I'm still learning things about her, and I've got a feeling that I could do that for the rest of my life and still not know her down to the core. There are so many layers to her, all of which I like and look forward to seeing more of. Everything from that sarcastic mouth to the parts of her that are most vulnerable.

"What's going on?" Dagger growls, throwing himself into one of the kitchen chairs. They'd come off shift last night. "I'll tell you what's going on." The flash of his teeth is a telling sign for my brother, and it's not a good one. He's pissed.

"Well, tell us," Gwyneth urges, cupping her coffee between both hands and readjusting in the chair with her feet in it.

Dagger glares at her and looks ready to strangle her if given the chance. He points his finger in Gwyneth's direction. "Get that friend of yours under control. Next time she tries one on with me . . ." he trails off, sneering. "Just get your friend in check.

"What did Angie do?" I ask, cocking a brow. No one has ever riled Dagger up like this.

"What didn't she do is more like it?" Dagger sneers, "Bitch called me—"

"Hey, don't go calling my best friend a bitch," Gwyneth snaps.

Dagger glowers. "Sorry, Gwenny," he mutters, calling her the name those who are friends of hers use.

For me, that's not the name I use. I like calling her Princess. It's a name only I use.

"It's okay, Dagger, now, what did Angie do?" Gwyneth sighs. "I know she can sometimes be a lot to handle."

It's all I can do to keep from snorting coffee out my nose at her choice of words. Angie is more than a lot. She's wacky and a bit out there. Pretty much, she's like Gwyneth but more open with what she blurts out.

"Damn woman called me in the middle of the night asking for a ride home 'cause she was drunk off her ass and didn't want to hear it from Ross," Dagger says, shaking his head. "I get to the bar she's at, and she's at a pool table with a bunch of other dudes hanging around takin' their money and pissin' 'em off at the same time. Anyway, when she sees me, she all but jumps me talking about how she wants to fuck me."

"And that's a bad thing?" I laugh.

"Stop it, Bruiser," Gwyneth says, giggling and swats at me, eyes focused on Dagger. "Well, did you? Fuck her, that is?"

Oh shit, she did not just ask that.

I look at the ceiling. I don't need her to know these details. Then again, she'd probably be hearing about it from Angie anyway.

"Fuck no, I didn't," Dagger all but shouts. "I carried her ass to her apartment, locked her inside, and put a prospect on her to make sure she didn't leave again."

"Okay, so I don't see what you need fixed." Gwyneth sets her coffee down and twirls her fingers in a circle. "What exactly do you need fixing?"

"Get back here ready to crash and find a text from her. It's a damn picture of her naked," he exclaims and points a finger at Gwyneth. "She's your friend. Got made respect for you, and she's damn cool people, but that shit ain't gonna fly. Fix it before I end up fixing it and hurting a damn good woman." With that said, my brother gets up and stomps through the apartment. "I'm gonna go take a shower. We going to the clubhouse today?"

"Yeah, brother, in just a little while. We've got church, and then I think Avery and Willow were doing some dinner thing," I answer, getting to my feet to get a refill.

"Right, let me know when y'all are ready." With that, he goes in the bathroom and closes the door behind him.

I turn my attention back to my woman to find her looking ready to laugh her ass off, but she is containing it so as not to piss off my already pissed brother.

"You gonna talk to her?" I ask, though I'm sure I already know the answer.

"Nope." Shaking her head, she smiles. "I'm not getting involved. If he doesn't want her in any way." Gwyneth pauses with a shrug. "It's his choice to make. I know my best friend, she wouldn't take kindly to me butting in. I get how she is and that she can come on strong. Especially if she's been drinking. She's ballsy and doesn't mind going for what she wants. Even when that person doesn't want the same. Way I see it, if he wanted her at all, he screwed up by not going there because she'll move on, and he will be a thing of the past."

"Weird way of letting a guy know she wants him." I don't get why women play games.

"How so? Guys pick up women they find attractive, why can't a woman?" She's got me there. "Angie's the type of woman that knows herself and what she likes in bed and out."

"I'll stop you right there," I tell her, holding my

hand up. "I don't need to hear what your best friend likes and doesn't like in the sack."

"Well, you asked, I was giving you an answer." Gwyneth smirks, gets up, and goes to the sink. I watch as she rinses her mug and sets it in the dishwasher. "Anyway, since we're going to the clubhouse, I'm going to go take my own shower."

She goes to walk by, but I pull her to me, "Want some company?" I ask, leaning in to brush my lips against hers. The thought of getting in that shower with her already has my dick throbbing.

"I highly doubt you have time."

Her breath hitches, and she presses deeper into me.

"Always have time for you, Princess. You want me to fuck you, I'll fuck you. Right here or in the shower."

"Hmm, I do like the idea," she murmurs and wraps her arms around my neck. "Why don't you join me in the shower and show me how you can use that giant monster of yours quickly."

Fucking hell. This woman was meant for me.

"Oh, baby, don't you worry. I'll show you what me and this giant monster can do to you, but it definitely won't be quick," I inform her, swooping her into my arms. I intend to make her scream, taking me deep inside her. I want her to be able to feel me the rest of the damn day, or at least until I can get back inside her.

"We've got a problem," Cy states no sooner than Hammer slams the gavel down.

"What kind of problem?" Malice asks, looking pissed already. His little girl hadn't wanted to let him go. She's a daddy's girl through and through. It didn't help that she'd been crying for him, and he'd had to put her off. That's something my VP doesn't like to do. His kids mean the world to him, just as Willow does. He nearly lost them all when he fucked up with Willow, but now he'd kill for them. Hell, we'd all kill to protect his kids, same with all of the other kids around here.

"Been watching for any signs of Johnathan Bryant showing himself. Not that I think it'll actually be him. From what I've found, and we all know already, he uses other people to do his dirty work," Cy states while sliding a file in my direction. "Late last night, Johnathan resurfaced. He did this by putting a reward out for the 'return of his property' on a site that's used to put hits out on people."

I open the file and scan over what exactly he's talking about, and my blood goes cold in my veins. "You've got to be joking. He's now focusing solely on Gwyneth."

"According to what I've been able to find, he's

washing his hands of Willow and Honor. They no long interest him at this time. At least that's what I've been told."

"By who?" Malice growls.

Cy sighs and shakes his head, glances around the table, pausing on Rogue for a moment, and then looks back to Malice and Hammer. "Rebel's receptionist. She reached out via an email address that was supposed to be anonymous, but she's not as sneaky as she thinks she is."

"The fuck is Alanna doing being your source?" Malice snarls, nostrils flaring.

I don't know Alanna that well, but she'd be around every once in a while with Willow. A while back, Malice and Hammer, with Willow's urging, got Alanna the job working for Rebel. I do know she's got her little sister she's raising and needed the job, but what I don't get is why the fuck she'd put herself in danger for something like this.

"Don't worry, VP, I made sure she didn't have anything trailing her through any back doors online," Cy states firmly. "But what she was able to send over is quite extensive. Johnathan doesn't want Willow now because she's protected far too well with the club and her grandfather's men."

"What about Honor?" Savage asks.

"She's got not just us but Glacier's club." Cy shrugs.

"I don't want to say this is all a good thing, he could end up still going after them, but as it stands right now, the bounty is out on Gwyneth. To make it all the sweeter," he spits out, curling his lip. "The amount is five mil with an order of kill to get to her."

Muffled curses can be heard around the table. This isn't good.

There'll be plenty of people out to claim the bounty.

"We're gonna have to take her to a safe house," I grunt, knowing it's the last thing she'll want.

"Agreed. Dagger and you'll move her out. Take her to one in Avon," Hammer orders.

"You want us to take her to the beach?" Not that I have a problem with it, but it's farther away from my brothers than I would like.

"Yeah, Twister's club won't be but a couple hours away. I'll call 'em and let them know what's going on."

I nod and look around the table. "That'll work, Prez, but any way Carbine and Colt can join us?"

"Yeah, that'll be good. A couple more eyes on her won't hurt, but y'all are going to have to leave tonight. The faster she disappears, the sooner we can have this taken care of." Hammer slams the gavel down, ending church, and the pit of my stomach feels like acid is building within it.

There's more to this than what we've found out.

This bastard is up to something. Something big. Whatever that is will bring on a reckoning none of us will be ready for, I'm sure of it. If something were to happen to Gwyneth, I know in my gut that I'll destroy anyone who gets in my way of those who dare touch her. She's mine, and I didn't even realize I could want a woman like her. That is until I laid eyes on her and got the reality check of a lifetime.

CHAPTER SEVENTEEN

GWYNETH

The look on Bruiser's face is enough to tell me whatever they discussed in church wasn't a good thing. I'm pretty sure it has to do with me.

Me and this situation that's happening with the man who is sick in the head.

I cross the room, meet him halfway, and plant my hands against his chest while his arms go around me. "What's going on?"

"We'll talk about it later. Right now, we gotta get back to the apartment, you need to pack a go-bag. We're heading out," he states, squeezing my waist.

I blink up at him, sensing now is not the time to argue with him about go-bag or about where we're going. So, instead, I lick my bottom lip and nod. "Okay, but you will tell me, right?"

"Yeah, Princess, I'll tell you," he mutters, dips his head down, and kisses me ever so gently. "Now, let's go."

"Okay." Stepping away from him, I don't get far before he snags me around the waist to keep me close. Together we make our way to where I left my stuff sitting while I spent time helping Avery and Willow with preparations. I grab my bag and smile at both women. "Sorry, we're not sticking around. I wish we could."

"It's okay," Avery says, looking somewhat upset. "When it comes to the club, I've learned to expect things like this."

"Trust us when we say it's never a dull moment around here," Willow adds to Avery's statement with a small smile. "If we didn't expect the unexpected around here, we'd all be running scared of the what-ifs and whatnots."

"Come on, Princess," Bruiser urges me toward the door, where I spot not only Dagger waiting but Colt and Carbine.

I nod and give both women a wave goodbye, a sense of dread twists around in my stomach, leaving me with a bad taste in my mouth. I'm used to just

Dagger and Bruiser watching out for me, but add in two more guys, there's more to whatever this is.

"Princess, we're heading out as soon as you get your bags packed," Bruiser says the moment we step over the threshold into the apartment. "We don't have time for explanations right now, but I swear once we're on the road, I'll give you the answers you deserve."

"Okay." I'm not surprised in the least, but it doesn't make me happy. I want to know what's going on. "Can you tell me how much I should pack?" I ask while pulling out a duffel bag from my closet.

"Just pack some clothes, Gwyneth. Whatever else you need, we'll pick up when we get where we're going. And you need to leave your phone here."

"I need to let Angie and her dad know I'm leaving town," I tell him, opening the bag. My mind whirling with the danger that I know I'm facing but not knowing what it is. I really want nothing more than to argue with him right now, though I know it's not a good idea. Not with the mood he's in.

"Gwyneth, baby, I know you want to talk to them and let them know, but you need to get packing and not worry about telling everyone where you're going.

We'll get word to them and let them know what's what. Now, get packed before I just throw shit in the bag for you." He turns and leaves the room without letting me speak further.

Biting back a response that might start an argument, I go about packing and throwing different random types of clothes in my bag. The last thing I go to grab is my birth control, and an idea pops in my head that has me grinning. I grab a couple of my toys, including my favorite one. I pack them quickly and throw a couple other things on top. I barely get the zipper zipped when Bruiser steps back into the room.

"Ready?" he asks, eyes going to my bag.

"Yes. Can you tell me now where we're going?" I ask, hefting my bag up off the bed.

Bruiser steps forward and takes the heavy bag from me. "I'll tell you when we get on the road."

"Right," I grumble, staring up at him. "Will you at least let me grab a few snacks from the kitchen? I don't want to have to rely on fast food and gas station junk."

"Already packed it up, Princess," he mutters. "Dagger's put it in the truck for me."

"Oh, um, okay. Well then, I'm ready."

Bruiser holds out his free hand. "Phone."

I bite back a curse, wishing he'd forget to ask about it, and walk over to where I'd tossed my purse on the couch and pull out my phone. "Here you go," I state a bit snappishly.

Taking the phone in his hand, he tosses it behind him on the side table, where it lands with a clatter. "Let's get moving," he orders, jerking his chin toward the door. "Dagger's already in the truck waiting for us."

"Why are we all riding in a truck?" I'm sure it seems like an annoying question to ask, but I need to know exactly what's going on. I don't like being in the dark.

"You, me, and Dagger are in the truck. Carbine and Colt are on their bikes. Mine and Dagger's bikes are in the trailer," he informs me while opening the door and stepping through, keeping me shielded.

"Why trailer the bikes?" I really wish he'd tell me what's going on. For that matter, when did they get a truck here with a trailer? This whole thing is starting to piss me off—more than just a little bit.

"In the truck, Princess. I'll tell you once we're in the truck."

"Fine, you better not leave anything out." I huff and follow his lead to the truck, where he opens the back door of the dual cab, tosses my bag in, turns to me, and hefts me up into my seat without so much as a grunt of response.

A moment later, he closes the door and rounds the hood to get in while Dagger hops into the passenger seat.

"Bikes are secure," Dagger remarks and turns to look behind him at me. "Don't worry about Grady. I made a call to him while waiting on you, explained a few things, and told him I'll be in touch."

"You talked to my captain without me even knowing first what's going on?" I snap, close to losing my temper.

"Princess," Bruiser takes on a totally new tone with me, one that not only seems like a warning, but seems like I'm nearly hitting the danger zone with him. His body is tense and his eyes are focused ahead of him on the road as he maneuvers the truck out of the parking lot and onto the road, heading in the direction of the interstate.

Why the hell does the song from *Top Gun* pop into my head? Like, seriously, if I don't get answers soon, I'm going to officially lose it.

"Don't Princess me, Dorian Tyler Bruiser Gentry," I all but snarl, using not only his road name but mixing it in with his real one because what the hell. "I deserve a damn answer as to what's going on."

"Yeah, you do, Gwyneth," Bruiser growls. "And I'll give them to you, but first, I'm trying to get us out of town before anyone is the fuckin' wiser. The last thing we need is for someone that wants to claim the bounty on your damn head to take their chance or follow us."

"What bounty?" I demand. My entire being seems to freeze all over.

"The one that was put out for you that's worth a shit ton to a lot of people," he grinds out. "Now, chill out. Give me just a little bit of time to get you the fuck out of here before I start telling you how this bastard is willing to pay five million to get his hands on you."

My stomach twists all the more, and I clamp my mouth shut. The blood in my veins goes cold, and a chill rushes over my body. Suddenly, I feel colder than I've ever felt in my life, including the time I spent in that godforsaken hellhole my mom sent me to.

Sitting back silently in my seat, I kick off my shoes, pull my legs up onto the seat, wrap my arms around them, press my cheek to my knees, and look out the window. There's nothing else I can say right now. Bruiser needs to focus, and I need to absorb the fact that some monster is willing to pay that much money for me.

Why? Why would someone be willing to pay such an amount? I'm having a hard time comprehending all of this. I need Bruiser to talk to me and explain what he knows, but not right now. He needs to focus on the road and make sure we get wherever it is we're going safely.

"Come on, Princess, we're here."

"Hmm," I murmur, feeling his big arms scooping me up out of the backseat where I'd fallen asleep at some point. I blink a couple times, seeing it was dark out, but I could hear the sound of waves splashing. "Where are we?" I don't bother lifting my head off his shoulder and simply snuggle deeper into him.

"One of the club's safe houses," he answers, backing away from the truck.

"We'll get all the bags," Dagger announces, keeping his voice quiet.

Bruiser grunts something, but I don't really hear him as I allow myself to drift off once again. With this man's arms around me, warmth starts to seep through the cold, and I feel safe when I know safety isn't something I should allow myself to feel right now.

"You gotta wake up, baby," Bruisers murmurs, not letting me completely fall asleep again. "I gotta make sure you eat something, then we're gonna finally talk."

"I don't wanna," I grumble sleepily. "Tomorrow."

"Gwyneth, we're not waiting until then."

I know that tone Bruiser's using and it's not one I'm willing to argue with. Honestly, I don't even have the energy to fight him on it.

Bruiser carries me up some stairs and into a house

already lit up. I'm guessing one of the other guys went ahead of us and opened the doors. Just inside the house, he lowers me to my feet and takes my hand. "Come on, I'll take you to the kitchen and make you something to eat while I tell you everything you need to know."

"Okay, Bruiser." I sigh, giving in to him. I wanted to know everything, but I didn't. In the truck just before falling asleep some time ago, I decided ignorance was bliss.

Bruiser guides me through, up another set of stairs, and it dawns on me we're at a beach house.

"Where exactly are we?" I ask him as we clear the stairwell and the open kitchen living space comes into view.

The kitchen is a nice size with stainless steel appliances, a curved counter in the middle with a sink surrounded by black granite tile. A long wooden light-grain table sits just off to the side of the kitchen. On the other side, there's a couch and loveseat squaring off another section of the space. The walls are a cool blue with different types of beach decor hanging, including a map. The back wall is mostly all windows except for a set of glass double doors, making the room feel bigger than it is. Granted, it's still a big room. I'm willing to bet in the light of day, it's a gorgeous space to be in.

"The club has several safe houses. Some in state. Some out. This one is in Avon and isn't just a safe house, it's used whenever one of the members wants to come to the beach," he says, moving around the kitchen and pulling things out to make sandwiches. "Our room is on the second floor, along with Dagger's. Carbine and Colt are going to take the bottom floor. There's a bathroom just behind the kitchen in that little adjacent hall."

"So, we're at a beach," I remark, moving to sit on a stool in front of him, watching him as he works at making a sandwich.

"Yep." He nods. "Hammer made a call to Twister, the president of the Franklin Charter. He found out Horse, the VP there, is actually in town with his family. They stocked up the place for us."

"That was nice of them."

"Yeah, it was," he says, lifting his gaze to mine, and I know it's time. He's going to tell me what he hadn't told me in the truck. "Johnathan Bryant put a bounty on you. One that says kill anyone who gets in the way."

And there it is. The reason we're in a safe house. We're all here because it's safer to be away from everyone else and not get anyone else hurt. This is far worse than I ever thought it could be. To make matters worse, Bruiser and his brothers are risking their safety to protect me, which scares me even more.

If something were to happen to any of them, especially Bruiser, I don't think I could handle it. I know for a fact I couldn't. In the time we've actually been together, he's come to mean so much to me, and it would kill me if he were gone.

CHAPTER EIGHTEEN

GWYNETH

I come awake to warm, strong arms surrounding me and the length of the man the arms are attached to pressing against me. Even better, the hard shaft sliding between my bare thighs.

Bruiser's awake, and more than ready to play, it seems. I, for one, wouldn't mind.

Last night, after we finished eating our sandwiches, I excused myself to take a shower and to think about everything he told me. It wasn't just the part about the bounty on my head. It was more to it. Stuff I'm doing my best not to think about.

After my shower, I curled up in the bed, not bothering to put any clothes on or drying my hair. I did at least lotion my skin, using some stuff I found in the bathroom. I couldn't be happier to have someone at least think to stock up with stuff we could actually use since I didn't get the chance to pack my bathroom essentials.

I'd fallen asleep before Bruiser came in the room, so I don't know when he joined me, but I definitely don't mind that he's here now. With nothing between us, he could easily slide inside me and take me just like this. But that's not what I want. No, I want something else entirely.

I pull away enough to roll over. I glance at Bruiser's face to find his eyes closed. Smiling, I press my lips to the center of his chest. He doesn't move, and I kiss him again, then again, moving downward. That is until I come to the part of him that I crave tasting the most. I wrap a hand around the base and lick my lips, eyes going up to find he's still yet to open his eyes. But I know he's awake. It's in the way he's holding his body still.

With a swirl of my tongue around the tip, I take my time to explore, bobbing my head, taking him nearly to my throat, and swallowing. I do this several times, drawing back, paying attention to just under the head of his shaft, and going back down to take him deep.

Bruiser groans and wraps his fingers in my hair,

taking control of my movements. I love the way he does this. It makes it all that much better.

"Fuckin' love your mouth, Princess," he rasps gruffly. His fingers tighten in my hair and it makes me that much hotter.

I slide my free hand between my thighs and circle my clit, moaning at the sensation it sends through my body. Needing more, I dip my fingers farther into my pussy, thrusting two deep inside. As good as it feels, I need more. I want more, but I like Bruiser's dick in my mouth. Remembering where my bag was, I draw away from him long enough to inch to the side of the bed.

"What you doing, Princess?" he asks, propping himself up.

"You'll see." I give him a grin and reach into my bag sitting next to the bed. Opening it, I wrap my fingers around the base of my dildo and pull it out. I meet Bruiser's heated gaze when he realizes what I have in my hand.

"Come here," he orders, not giving me a chance to do just that. He reaches for me, grips my waist, turns, and lifts me until I'm straddling him, his face between my legs. "Give me that toy," he commands, holding a hand out for the dildo. I give it to him without so much as a peep. This is exactly what I want.

Not waiting for him, I lower myself down and take his length back in my mouth. This time sucking him enthusiastically, wanting to taste him. It becomes harder to focus on my own task when Bruiser not only uses the toy but his mouth.

Back and forth, he fucks me with the toy and sucks my clit until I'm moaning around his shaft. We battle each other to give the most pleasure we can.

He beats me at it when he adds fingers to press into my rear. It's something he's done a few times, but not like this. First, one finger, then another. There's something to be said about him taking me like this, filling me so completely.

The need to come is nearly too much to bear, but I'm not to be outdone. Taking him to my throat, I swallow and hum, at the same time cupping his balls, toying with them.

Unfortunately for me, no matter how much Bruiser groans and enjoys what I do to him, he's better at it. Way better, but in the next moment, he has me coming and crying out around his shaft. He pulls the dildo from my pussy and replaces it with his mouth lapping up my juices. What I didn't expect was for him to press the dildo to my rear. I freeze for all of a second before he distracts me, making me lose my mind.

With each thrust into my rear, he drives his tongue into my entrance. I love every bit of it, even if I'm unsure if I should. He does this until I'm filled entirely and presses the button on the end of the dildo, turning the vibrations on. There's no stopping the scream that leaves me. I jerk and buck against the thing, uncertain what he's doing to me.

Even more so when Bruiser flips us, comes up between my thighs, and thrusts halfway inside me. "Fuckin' hell, Gwyneth, love this pussy. Just the taste of it is enough to make me an addict. It's more so when I'm fuckin' you," he groans, pulls out, and thrusts home. The dildo in my ass makes it that much tighter around him and causes so much sensation, I don't know if I can handle it all. "Swear that fake dick in your ass was a beautiful sight, but feeling how tight you are around me feels even better."

"Oh God, Bruiser. Please fuck me. I need you to fuck me. No more playing." I sink my nails into his shoulders and hold on tight.

"Don't worry, Princess, I've got you."

And got me, he does. Jerking my legs up, he does exactly what I need him to. Fucks me hard. Fucks me with long strokes that have tingles racing along my spine. My orgasm just over the horizon rushes me with such intensity that it leaves me breathless when it hits me.

"Damn right, baby, come all over my dick." He growls, picks up the pace, hurtling me into another release. It feels amazing, and I love it. Every bit of it.

Especially when he snarls my name, his release spilling from him, destroying me yet solidifying just how much he means to me. It takes a lot of trust for me to allow him to do what he did, and truth be told, I want him to do it over and over again.

"You gonna let me up anytime soon?" Bruiser asks a while later after not only taking the dildo from my ass but cleaning it and me. He then rejoined me in the bed, where I all but curled up on top of him.

"Nope," I remark, snuggling against his chest. "I'm good right here."

"I could be good too, Princess, but sometime or another, I've got to get up and check on things," he says, bursting my pretty little bubble I didn't realize I'd allowed myself to put around us. I was able to pretend for just a bit that nothing was wrong. "Besides, if I'm gonna fuck you like that again, I'm gonna need some substance in me. Sandwiches from last night have definitely been worn off."

My stomach takes the moment to make itself known quite loudly at that.

"Seems I need to make sure you're fed too." Bruiser chuckles and swats at my tender bottom. "Come on, Princess, I'll make you something to eat.

You can sit out on the back deck and enjoy the view for a while."

"If I must." I sigh, not wanting to move, but both of us need to eat. And a cup of coffee wouldn't be turned down.

Bruiser's chuckle switches to a laugh as he rolls us out of the bed. "Get dressed, baby."

"Yeah, yeah," I grumble, roll my eyes, and walk around the bed to where my bag is. I dig through and pull out a pair of panties, a bra, a pair of leggings, and a tank top with the Primal Fitness logo on it. I quickly dress and grab my brush, flip my hair upside down, and run it through my hair, getting the tangles out.

Hands at either side of my hips is the only way I know Bruiser has moved. "Damn fine sight," he utters and presses into my rear.

"We didn't have to get up, you know," I say, finishing with my hair. I straighten, making sure my hair doesn't hit him in the face.

"Yeah, but then we'd perish away without the food I intend to feed you." He chuckles, presses a kiss to the side of my neck, and steps back. "You done getting dressed?"

"I was just going to throw my hair up, but other than that, yeah."

"Don't worry about your hair. Leave it down," he

states, reaching out to brush his fingers through my hair. "I like it down."

I don't mind having it down either, so I don't mind him telling me to leave it like this.

"If you're gonna feed me, then you better get on it," I inform him before I decide to jump him and have my wicked way with him, which could end up with him driving me insane with pleasure once again.

CHAPTER NINETEEN

BRUISER

"Any news?" I ask, speaking to my brothers, though my attention is on the woman sitting outside on one of the reclined wooden chairs, drinking her coffee.

"Someone broke into her apartment last night and met the end of Ruger's fist," Dagger answers. "Glock reported seeing two unknowns around the station, and Grady said he got a call from someone he didn't know looking for Gwyneth."

"I talked to Blade. He's posted himself at the gym and reported seeing someone there looking for her," Colt remarks, grimacing and lowering his voice. "He also noted the person showing interest in Angie. I think someone needs to look out for her."

Shit. We should have put someone on Angie from

the get-go. The woman is an easy target to get to Gwyneth. If they get their hands on Angie, she's the perfect bait in order to draw Gwyneth out. Or the use of Simon, but we've ensured he's disappeared. No one can find him. At least not easily.

"Get that woman out of sight," Dagger grumbles, nostrils flaring.

"Blade's already on it," Carbine murmurs, rolls his shoulders, and rocks his head side to side, his neck popping. "We need to get some new damn beds in that room I'm in. It's too damn uncomfortable."

"You'll survive," I grunt as my cell buzzes in my pocket. Wondering who it is, I pull it out and groan. I'd forgotten to let my sister know I'd be out of town. "Hold on a sec," I tell my brothers and answer the call. "Leanna, you okay? The kids?" I hadn't spent much time with any of them since the funeral, nor had I gone anywhere near them with the threat to Gwyneth. I didn't want to put them in the path of danger.

"Yeah, I'm okay," she says, not sounding quite like herself. "I was just calling 'cause I wanted to let you know the insurance money came in from Mom's policy. She left it to both of us—"

"Take my half and use it for those kids," I interrupt her, not wanting anything to do with the money. I don't need it, and I hate the idea of taking money from my mom's death.

"Are you sure?" Leanna asks after a moment's pause.

"I'm sure. There anything else?"

"Well, I was going to see if you wanted to come for dinner, but from the tone of your voice, you're busy."

Closing my eyes, I drop my head back and take a breath. "If I were in town, I'd do dinner, Lele, but I'm not in town right now. Some serious shit's going down, and you need to stay clear of the clubhouse for the time being. Unless Hammer sends one of the members to come get you, don't go near it."

"Umm, okay," she murmurs. "You're not going to tell me why, are you?"

"You know I'm not," I grunt.

"Right, then, does it have anything to do with the pretty paramedic that treated Mom and was at the funeral?"

I didn't even think she noticed Gwyneth at the funeral. Straightening my head once more, I open my eyes to look out on the back deck to where my woman is sitting, watching the ocean waves crash against the shore.

"Yeah, I'll give you that much, and when all this is over, I'll introduce you to Gwyneth."

At the mention of her name, Gwyneth turns in her chair to meet my gaze.

"Gwyneth is a really pretty name. I look forward to

meeting her. Mom would be happy you finally found someone. Let me know when you're back in town, and the coast is clear. We'll do dinner." With that, Leanna disconnects.

Sighing, I pull the phone from my ear and shove it back into my pocket. My sister always likes getting the last word in. She'll stay clear for the time being, but it seems when this is all over, she'll want to meet Gwyneth pronto.

"Leanna okay?" Dagger asks.

"Yeah, insurance money came in," I tell him, shaking my head.

"Right." Dagger nods, understanding where I'm coming from. "She going to listen and stay clear of the clubhouse?"

"You know she will. When it comes to those kids, she's like a damn lioness and will do whatever it takes to protect them." I shrug. "Now, back to it . . ." My eyes are glued to Gwyneth while my brothers and I finish going over what we need to do in order to keep her safe. The whole time, she sits out on the deck, having returned her attention back to the scenery.

I need to talk to her, fill her in so she knows, but she seems to be enjoying herself, and I don't want to ruin it for her. Regardless, she's gonna need to know about Angie. I won't keep that from her. She has a right to know, and I've seen Gwyneth teaching self-defense. I know when it comes down to helping me protect her, she can do it. Granted, I'm hoping it doesn't come down to that.

My brothers and I finish our conversation, with Colt and Carbine going back to sleep. They'll stay up through the night to keep guard while the rest of us sleep.

Thoughts of being in the bed with Gwyneth, my dick thickens. This morning with her in the bed, taking her the way I did, using that damn toy, working it in her ass while I fucked her pussy. I don't think I've ever had a woman cream for me the way she did. It was hotter than anything I've ever experienced, and I look forward to seeing if I can get her even hotter. I want to see her burn brighter for me, but I don't want my brothers around to hear her screams of pleasure as I know they did this time.

"You gonna go out there and sit with your woman or stare at the back of her head?" Dagger snorts, moving to the couch and flopping down on it, nabbing the remote. "Let me know if we're going anywhere. Otherwise, game's on and I'm watching it."

"Which game?"

The sweetest sound of Gwyneth's voice fills my ears as I find her coming back inside.

"USC is playing Michigan, later VMI is up against

Cavaliers," Dagger answers and looks over his shoulder. "Baseball."

"Sweet, I like USC, but I also like Duke."

"Duke has a good team, but I gotta say East Carolina is better. But LSU is my team."

"LSU is definitely the team to beat," Gwyneth says, finding a spot on the loveseat, eyes coming to me. "You going to stand there, or we watching a game?"

"We're watching the game, Princess." I grin, liking the fact I found a woman who likes baseball. Between baseball and football, those are the two sports I enjoy watching. Mostly college rather than professional.

Rounding the loveseat, I scoop Gwyneth up and turn, getting comfortable with her in my arms, eyes on the TV screen and the game just starting. Here's to a day at the beach, relaxing and watching baseball.

I'll wait until later to fill her in. Let her have this time to enjoy a day of peace.

CHAPTER TWENTY

BRUISER

The vibration of my phone on the nightstand wakes me. Not wanting it to wake Gwyneth, I reach out, snatch it up, and crack an eye open in order to see who the hell's calling.

Seeing Hammer's name on the screen, I answer and put the phone to my ear.

"Yeah, Prez?"

"Get Gwyneth back here ASAP," he orders.

"Why? What's happened?" I ask, jolting out of the bed.

"Someone found Simon. Don't know how, but he's dead."

"Fuck," I snarl, waking Gwyneth up.

"Bruiser?" Her voice sleep-filled, and her expression is one of concern.

"Hang on, baby," I tell her, focusing on the conversation with Hammer. "How'd it happen?"

"Decapitation."

Fuck. Fuck. Fuck.

"You need to get her back here where we can lock her down. If they found him, who wasn't supposed to be able to be found, they can get to her," Hammer states, sounding pissed. Far more than I've heard him sound in a while. Even when we went up against Avery's siblings, who wanted him out of the way to get to her. "And Bruiser . . ."

"Yeah?"

"They left a message behind. Saying the men protecting her were next."

"I'll let the others know and break it to her," I tell him and disconnect, my mind racing with this news. It seems Johnathan has gone and lost it. I drop my phone to the floor, grab my jeans from the floor, and yank them on. "Get up, Princess. I need you dressed and ready to go in the next few minutes."

"What's happening?" she asks, a slight tremble in her voice.

Slowly taking a breath, I release it and move to her side of the bed. Sitting down, I pull her into my arms. "I've got something to share with you, Princess, and it's not good. I want to be able to give you time to process it when I do, but I can't. We've got to get on the road. Okay?"

"Okay." She nods, her voice no more than a breath. "Just tell me."

Giving her a squeeze, I press a kiss to her forehead. "That was Hammer on the phone. He called to let me know . . ." Sucking in a harsh breath, I lay the news on her. "Gwyneth, someone found Simon. He's dead, baby."

Gwyneth draws in a sharp breath, eyes filling with tears. "How?"

"Princess, you don't want to know," I murmur, palming the side of her face and stroking her cheek with my thumb. "Trust me, it's not something you want to know. Now, I really need for you to get ready, we're heading out. Taking bikes out of here, and I've got to tell the others."

Gwyneth allows a single tear to fall, and she nods. I wish I could give her time to grieve, but it'll have to come later.

I kiss her forehead and finish dressing quickly, while she also gets her stuff together. We're on the back of my bike, but she didn't overpack. I'll be able to put the small duffel in one of the saddle bags.

Needing reassurance she's gonna be okay, I pull her in my arms, wrapping them tightly around her, and press a kiss to her forehead. "You gonna be okay?"

Gwyneth nods in answer, her breath hitching.

I press another kiss to her forehead, step back, and drop my hands from around her waist. "I'll be right back, Princess."

"Okay," she whispers, the tears she's holding back could be heard in her voice.

One last look in her direction, I go bang on Dagger's door. "We gotta roll," I shout for him to hear me. I don't wait for him to open his door before going in search of the other two. I find Colt on the back deck and Carbine in the kitchen. "Get your shit. We're heading out. Hammer called we gotta get back to the clubhouse. Taking the bikes."

"What's happened?" Dagger asks, coming in, eyes alert, hair disheveled.

"Gwyneth's brother was found, killed, and a message was left behind," I tell 'em. "We got to get back to the clubhouse. We need to get there without someone seeing or catching us before we arrive."

"How the fuck did they find him?" Carbine demands, nostrils flaring.

"What message did they leave?" Colt asks, his voice that of steel.

I glance toward the stairs, making sure Gwyneth isn't in hearing distance before answering. "That we're next."

"Fuckin' hell," Dagger snarls and rakes a hand through his hair. "I'll get my shit."

"We leave in five," I tell him.

"I'll meet you at the bikes." Dagger nods and darts off back to his room.

"We'll go unload yours and Dagger's bikes from the trailer," Colt announces.

"Appreciate it," I grunt and head back to my room to find Gwyneth coming out, face paler than I've ever seen it.

Without even thinking, I move to her and pull her in my arms, where she burrows her face in my chest. "If I could change what happened, I would in a heartbeat, Princess."

"I know you would, Bruiser," she says, her words muffled.

Cupping the back of her head, holding her to me, I give her the support she needs from me. I know it's not enough, but for now, it'll have to do.

"We've got to get on the road," I tell her.

"Yeah." Nodding, she takes a step back, drawing from my arms. "I'm ready when you are. You can leave my bag here if we need to."

"Grab it, baby, we'll stow it in my saddlebag. You don't have anything at the clubhouse, so it'll give you something until we can get you more." I don't know how long she's going to be locked down, but until this shit is handled, I'm not taking any chances. We get her in the club, then I'll find the motherfucker who's responsible for not only the bounty but also the death of Gwyneth's brother. Then I'm gonna make sure he screams before I take his head the way Gwyneth's brother lost his.

"We got anything new?" I ask Hammer the moment we step into the clubhouse. My hand tight around Gwyneth's, keeping her close. She's been damn good about all this since finding out about her brother, but I know at some point she's gonna break. When she does, I want to be there for her, however, she needs me.

"Savage and Gunner are on their way back. They didn't report much over the phone," Hammer informs me and looks at my woman, eyes filling with compassion. "Gwyneth, I'm sorry about your brother."

"It's okay," she whispers, and from the tears in her eyes, I know it's not.

"Babe, it's not okay," Hammer mutters and shakes his head. "None of this is okay. Your brother shouldn't have been killed. You shouldn't be targeted. Unfortunately, we live in a world that's unfair and pretty fucked-up. I lost my brother and his wife to this life.

Not the MC but the dark side of our lives. A satanic cult killed them, left my nephew in their blood, and took my niece. So, I know what you're feeling, even if it's a different type of feeling. Losing a sibling isn't like a parent. They grow up with you. They're your best friend even when they're not. You lose a part of yourself when you lose them, but darlin' you gotta remember something . . ." He pauses, a look of tormented grief on his face. "You gotta remember, no matter what, they're still with you every day. You got the memories to keep 'em alive. No one can take those from you."

"Thank you, Hammer." Tears stream down Gwyneth's face, and I don't think she's even aware of them.

"Not a problem, Gwenny." Hammer gives a curt nod and looks at me. "Soon as Savage and Gunner get here, we'll converge in church and discuss what's going on and what the plan is."

"Got it, Prez." Taking that as my cue, I guide Gwyneth farther into the clubhouse, taking her to a table. "I'm gonna get you a cup of coffee, Princess."

"Okay."

She doesn't look up at me as she takes a seat. Her eyes seem haunted and focused on something not in front of her.

Leaning down, I press a kiss to the top of her forehead. I keep her in my peripheral while I head to where the coffee sits ready behind the bar. Dagger, Colt, and Carbine all have mugs in hand as they move away to give me room.

"She's gonna be okay," Dagger states. "I sent Hammer a text at the last stop while we were filling the bikes up asking if he minded if I made a call. He didn't, so I did once we got here. They should be here any minute."

I know precisely who he's talking about and nod my gratitude.

No sooner than I take my seat next to Gwyneth, the door is thrown open, and not only do both Grady men and Angie come rushing in, but a woman who looks so much like Angie, I knew it was her mother. The four of them set their sights on Gwyneth. The men's expressions were stormy, the women's filled with concern.

Gwyneth gets to her feet, and I follow suit, wrapping an arm around her shoulders, holding her, and giving her the warmth and strength she needs.

"Oh, my sweet girl," the older woman rushes Gwyneth, pulling her out of my arms.

I take a step back as the others surround her. Seeing the way, they'd taken her into their family hits a part of me, and I know she deserves every bit of what they're giving her. The love of a family that should have always been, rather than the one she grew up with. Losing Simon, her only blood relation hit her hard, and I know it.

"It's gonna be okay, sweetheart," Grady murmurs, pressing a kiss to the top of her head, his gaze coming to mine.

I give him a curt nod, giving them some space, but not taking her away from them.

After a few moments, Gwyneth steps back, and I'm there to wrap an arm around her. I'll do what I can to give to her right now. Later on, I'll take care of her in other ways, but for now, this'll have to do until after I meet with my brothers and find out what the game plan is going to be.

My thought . . . go to the damn source of it all. Confront the woman who allowed all of this to happen in the first damn place. I wonder if Gwyneth's parents even know about the death of their son. Hell, I wonder if the father even knows any of this.

The way Gwyneth and Simon made it seem is that he's oblivious to it all. Materialistic, just as the mother.

Maybe it's time to give him a visit on top of dealing with his wife in the process.

CHAPTER TWENTY-ONE

GWYNETH

The thought of my brother being gone leaves an ache in my chest that won't go away. I never thought I'd lose him like this. Never in my life did I think I would have to deal with my brother's death. I get we all die at some point in our lives . . . it's that he's gone at such a young age. It's hard to fathom.

I keep wondering what his last thoughts were. Did he see it coming? Was he scared? Did he feel pain? Or was it a slow death?

I know I need to come to terms with this and that I'll never have answers to any of my questions, but it doesn't make the pain go away.

"Princess, why don't you sit down," Bruiser murmurs, squeezing my shoulder.

I nod and let him guide me back to where we'd been sitting before Angie and her family got here. I couldn't be more grateful to the Gradys for coming and the club for letting them. With everything going on, I didn't think they'd allow them on the property, but they did. And with what Hammer shared with me about his brother, I sense more than ever he knows exactly what I'm feeling. Just as Bruiser does, considering his mother passed away. But it's different in so many ways. She wasn't killed. Simon was.

"Bruiser," Hammer shouts from across the room, and I glance in the direction to find him motioning for Bruiser to join them.

"I'll be back, baby," Bruiser says, grips my chin, and forces me to meet his gaze. "Stay here, or if you want, go to my room." He places a key in my hand. "Just don't go outside. You need me. I'll be in church, but all you gotta do is knock on the door, and someone will open it."

"Okay," I whisper, nodding, not wanting him to leave me. Having his arm around me makes me feel safe and secure, losing them will leave me cold, but I know they've got to talk.

Bruiser gets directly in my face, nose pressed into mine. "Seriously, Gwyneth, you need me, knock, and I'll come out. I don't want to leave you alone, but know this, Princess, you're not alone. You've got your best friend and her family here with you. You got the ol' ladies watching you like they want to wrap you in bubble wrap and shield you from the world."

"I'll be okay, Bruiser, I promise," I tell him, reaching up to touch his cheek. "If I need you, I'll come get you." Though I won't, he doesn't need me to bother him when he needs to focus. Plus, I have Angie here, her and the rest of her family.

"All right, baby." He presses a kiss to my lips and straightens. "I'll be back as soon as I can." Leaving me, I watch him until he disappears into the room with his brothers following suit.

"I like him," Mrs. Grady announces.

"Of course you do, Mom." Angie giggles and rolls her eyes before focusing on me as she takes my hand. "I'm really sorry about Simon, Gwenny. I wish I could do something for you."

"I know you do, and I wish you could." My breath hitches in my chest. It's hard to breathe from the pain of the loss.

"Sweetheart," my captain calls, reaching across the table to take my hand in his and squeezes. "There's no taking the pain away, darlin', but in time it'll ease. It's not like with the job. In our field of work, you know we deal with death, but we lock it away and keep going. We don't think about it again. That's what we tell each other, though, the memory never goes away, we just keep truckin', knowing we'll do everything we can to save the next one. Unfortunately, when you lose someone close to you, a sibling, a daughter, a son, or a parent, it's never the same. What you need to remember is Simon loved you, Gwyneth. He loved you as any brother could. All he wanted to do was protect you."

Tears stream down my face as I nod, my lip trembling. "Has . . . has anyone told our parents?"

"I don't think so, but I'm sure they're going too," he answers, giving my hand another squeeze. "You don't think about them right now. Just worry about you and you alone."

"How are things with Bruiser?" Angie asks, changing the subject to something I like much prefer talking about.

I give her a smile. "They're good. I think I'm in love with him," I admit.

"I think if you two are going to talk about this, I'm going to the kitchen and see if I can help in making dinner or something," Angie's mom says.

"I think I'll join you," Captain Grady grumbles.

"I'm gonna get a beer. I don't need to hear this shit," Ross grunts. He stands, walks around the table, and presses a kiss to the top of my head before murmuring, "He might have been your brother and he loved you, but you're a part of this family too. You're like a sister to me, and I don't like seeing you hurting. When you hurt, I hurt. That's what it means to be a brother, and I know Simon felt the same way. And for the record, Bruiser hurts you, and I'll put a hurting on him."

I can't help but giggle, even with tears running down my cheeks. "Thank you, Ross," I whisper.

"Anytime, Gwenny," he says and leaves me alone with Angie.

The two of us aren't left alone for long, though. Avery, Willow, and Rebel take their place.

"I know you probably don't want it or need it, but we want you to know we're all here for you. CJ and Zinnia wanted to come over here too, but they're in the kitchen still working on putting together something to eat for everyone. Honor's at work right now, otherwise, she'd also be here," Avery rambles, fidgeting in her seat.

"We didn't want to crowd you," Willow also adds.

"If you need me to do anything. Look into any legal matters regarding your brother, just let me know," Rebel states, reaching out to grip my hand.

"Thank you, Rebel," I say, giving her a small smile. "I really appreciate it."

"Now, what's this about you being in love with Bruiser?" Angie says, getting back to the topic at hand.

"You're in love with Bruiser?" Avery asks beaming. "This is great!"

"Totally great," Willow agrees, nodding.

"I don't know how to explain what I'm feeling. Just that when it comes to Bruiser, I know he means everything to me. When he lost his mom, I blamed myself for not being able to not only save her but also not to be able to take away his pain."

"You know we did everything we could," Angie remarks. "And I can tell you that man, he has some very strong feelings for you, babe. The way he stood close when we first got here and Mom hugged you, then took you back in his arms. That's not even including the way he acted any other time I've been around him. From day one, he's totally been into you."

For the next couple of hours, these women have kept me from spiraling and even made me laugh a time or two. Eventually, Angie's mom and the other ol' ladies joined us and bought with them a bottle of Jack. CJ claimed nothing helped ease pain the way Jack Daniels does.

By the time the men stepped from church, I was three sheets to the wind, telling the women a story about a call Angie, Mick, and I went on where a guy had his junk stuck on a PVC plumbing pipe that had sealant on it. The guy had all but glued himself to the thing. I don't even know what had been in his mind about doing something so idiotic.

All of us are giggling when Bruiser comes up behind me and shifts my hair off one of my shoulders.

"You doin' okay, Princess?" he asks, dips his head down, and presses a kiss to the side of my neck.

"Better with the help of Jack," I answer, tilting my head back to meet his gaze.

"I see that," he says, watching me closely. "We're heading out for a bit, you gonna be okay without me?"

"Where are you going?" The question is out before I can stop it.

"This shit, baby, I'm not about to let it keep happenin'. We're ending this shit once and for all." His eyes flash in anger. "I'll be back in a while. When you get tired, I want you in my bed. Okay?"

I lick my bottom lip, drawing it between my teeth, nodding.

"Good." Leaning into me, he kisses me. "Be back."

"Okay."

I keep my gaze on him as he backs away and stalks through the clubhouse, his brothers with him. I don't know what they're planning or going to do, but I hope whatever it is they're going to do, they come back safe and unhurt. I don't think I could handle him or anyone else being hurt because of the threat to me.

A part of me wants to just give up and find this

monster and give myself over in order to save everyone else. However, the reasonable part of me knows I can't do that. If I do, my life is over.

I have to trust Bruiser and the others. I saw the look in his eyes. Whatever or whoever he's about to face off with tonight, they don't know what they're up against. They're in for one hell of a reckoning when it comes to that man. He's not one to be trifled with.

CHAPTER TWENTY-TWO

BRUISER

The first real-time I've seen my woman get shit-faced shouldn't have been because she's dealing with the death of her brother. It pisses me off that I'm leaving her alone as it is. Her being drunk off her ass, yeah, that doesn't make me happy. Not in the least.

During church, my brothers and I all came to an agreement. This shit comes to an end. To get to Johnathan Bryant, we're going to confront the threat that started it all. Not completely, since he was already after Willow and using Honor as a way of bait through Simon. How the wheels have turned. He doesn't want the others anymore.

We'll still be taking him out as well, but first up, Gwyneth's parents. More or less, her mother. Neither of them knows about Simon, or they shouldn't that is. It'll be interesting to see the news dawning on them when they find out. If, from what we know about the mother, she won't be a blubbering mess. What I want to see for myself is how the father will react to the knowledge his son is dead. Will he be torn up about it like his daughter? Will he wonder where his daughter is? If she knows? How she's taking the news?

Riding with my brothers now, I can't get the sight of Gwyneth's heart breaking out of my head. All I keep seeing is the pain filling her eyes. The tears wanted to escape the hold she'd had on them. Her pain echoed out to me. Fuck me, I never want to see that look in her expression again.

The more I think about it, the higher my anger gets. It's time for the bullshit to be done and over with. By the end of the night, I swear one way or another, this shit ends for my woman. I won't allow anything else to happen to her.

Enough is enough.

The people behind this, the ones responsible . . . they're in for a reckoning they've never seen before. I'll take them all down and burn their homes to the ground.

Thirty minutes pass, and soon we're driving up to a gated property. Cy does his thing and gets the gate to open. Once we're through, we ride right up to the front doors.

The door opens immediately to two men who look similar to each other, even though one is much older than the other. Father and son. Simon and Gwyneth's father and grandfather. Both of them are dressed in suits that look like they cost about what I spent on all of my leather together.

"What the dickens is going on here?" the grandfather demands the moment all of us shut our bikes off.

No one replies to the old man as we climb off the back of our bikes and make our way toward them.

"I'll have you all arrested for trespassing," the old coot blusters.

"You go ahead and try to have us arrested, you old bastard," Malice snarls. "I'd like to see you try."

I guess my VP knows the older man.

"Who are you people, and what are you doing here?" Gwyneth's father asks, and on a closer look, I can see some resemblance.

"I'm your daughter's man," I speak up, stepping forward. "Do you have any idea the bullshit you and your wife have caused? That the debt your wife and you have caused is the reason your very own son is dead."

"Excuse me?" the old coot huffs.

"What are you talking about?" Gwyneth's father

asks, shock overtaking his expression. "What do you mean my son is dead? What have you done to him?"

"How about you ask your wife?" Hammer advises. "Speaking of her, where is she this evening?" Moving forward, he pushes his way through the two men into the oversized house.

"I'm calling the police," the old man shouts.

"Go ahead. Maybe they'd like to know how your son and his wife are behind your grandson's murder." Malice sneers.

"Why do you keep saying we're the reason? What have you done to my son? Where is my daughter?"

"Your daughter is none of your concern," I snap and get directly in his face. "Because of you and your wife's selfishness, not taking care of your debts the proper way and then not taking care of the money you owe that person, her life was put in danger. And your son, we hid, unfortunately, someone found him and killed him."

"We're not in debt," Gwyneth's father utters the words, taking a step back, his face paling. "I don't know what you're talking about. I don't know anything about this. Our finances are in order, and if they were in trouble, I would know about it and take care of things properly. I might be a lot of things, but I'm no fool when it comes to my money."

"You're an idiot and a sad excuse for a father," I

state, though I believe him when he says he's no fool when it comes to finances. "How about you explain to us then how your wife came to be in debt and seeking money from a man named Johnathan Bryant?"

This is something I want him to explain. And from the look on his face, he's not exactly thrilled to hear Johnathan's name.

"What is this about?" the old coot demands, stepping closer to his son. "We have nothing to do with the likes of Johnathan Bryant. He's nothing but trouble. Always has been."

"So, you know who this fucker is?" I quip.

"Oh, we know who he is," Gwyneth's father confirms, nodding curtly. "Come on inside, we'll discuss this in the other room and not in the foyer."

Following the other man, I take in the house where my woman grew up. Not a house. A fucking mansion that holds no personality whatsoever.

"My wife is out of town for one of her girl trips to some resort or somewhere with her friends according to the message she left for me with my receptionist."

The older man takes a seat in one of the high-back chairs as his son makes this announcement. "Woman is always looking to go to the spa or some other resort. She likes to spend money every chance she can."

"How about you explain to us how it is you know

nothing of a debt that has your name attached to your wife's?" Hammer demands.

Gwyneth's father doesn't bother looking toward my Prez, he keeps his gaze focused on me. "Gwyneth is safe? She's unharmed?"

"Don't concern yourself with my woman," I advise him. "And answer my Prez's question."

"I don't know what this debt is. If my wife has accrued this, then it is on her and her alone."

"That would be where you're wrong." Dagger snarls.

"Because of your wife, Gwyneth has a bounty on her head. A deal was struck that she would be used as payment for a debt to Johnathan Bryant," I inform her father and grandfather, meeting both of their gazes. "We have proof of communication between your wife and this fucker. Because of this debt, your son was killed. Someone cut his head off and left a message for anyone who protects Gwyneth that they're next."

"Oh God," Gwyneth's father utters, collapsing onto a chair behind him. "She did it," he mumbles to himself, shaking his head. "She really did it. She said she'd make me pay one day."

"Want to enlighten the rest of the class?" Gunner snaps.

"Gwyneth's mother . . . she died. We were having an affair when I found out she was pregnant with my daughter. I intended to leave my wife for her. Then, during childbirth, there were complications. She died, bled out. I stayed with my wife under the circumstances she were to act like a mother to my daughter, and we never tell her the truth."

"She knows your wife isn't her mother," I inform him.

"Of course she does. My daughter isn't stupid. I don't know what happened for her to leave the moment she could, but my wife, well, she said it was for the best. That it was what my little girl wanted."

"She left because your wife tormented her, and sent her off to some bullshit spa," I spit out and glare at both men. "Are you two oblivious to the fact the bitch was all but torturing her those six months that she was supposedly overseas studying? Fuckin' bitch was having her tormented by electrodes telling her she wasn't proper material for someone of your station. Because of her, Gwyneth slept in her car until her captain took her in. To make it all worse, your son was dragged into this, and to protect his sister, he tried going up against us. Then, he told his sister what was going down, and she had the sense to come to us and explain. Got her brother to explain. Got him to apologize. Because of her we did what we could to protect him. If not for your wife, none of this would have happened." By the time I finish, I'm shouting loud enough for the chandelier in the middle of the room to shake.

"Oh dear Lord," the older man whispers, face drained of all color.

"You want to make things better, start talking. Where exactly is your woman because she's definitely not at some spa," Malice states.

"I don't know. But I can call her."

"Don't do that," Cy interrupts Gwyneth's father. "Give me all of her phone numbers. Along with those she associates with."

For the next fifteen minutes, both men give us everything they know of.

By the time they finish, I'm itching to get back to Gwyneth. To make sure she's okay.

"Do you think I could possibly see my daughter?"

I glare at the man who fathered my woman. "I'll discuss it with her. See what she wants. You don't get anywhere near her unless I'm there, but more importantly, unless she wants to see you."

"Fair enough," the other man nods in agreement. "Please let her know that I'm truly sorry and that if she'll give me another chance, I'll make things right."

I grunt out an answer as my phone vibrates in my pocket. I pull it out to find it's a text from my sister. I open the message to make sure it's not an emergency, and my blood freezes in my veins just as my brothers also pull out their phones.

There's a text with a picture.

I have something you want. You have something I want. Trade, and they won't get hurt. I'd hate to take another head, but I will.

The picture was of my sister and her kids. All of them staring at the camera in fear, tears running down their cheeks.

Motherfucker.

CHAPTER TWENTY-THREE

BRUISER

"We need to go," I snarl, shoving the phone back in my pocket and slashing a glare at Gwyneth's father. If I lose my sister, this shit is on him. I'll kill him along with anyone else that gets in my way.

"Brother, we got to assume this wasn't just sent to us," Hammer says far too calmly.

"Oh, I'm willing to bet it was sent to the women as well," I snarl and stomp to my bike. I struggle to lock down the rage wanting to take over. I need my head right now. Also don't need my brothers to lock my ass up to keep me under control.

"I want half of you going to the clubhouse, secure the women and kids. Lock them together in one of the rooms, and don't let them out. The rest of you, we're going to Bruiser's sister's house," Hammer yells.

My phone buzzes, this time alerting me to a phone call. I pull it out as I straddle my bike and find it's my woman calling. I take a deep breath to calm my ass down and answer. "You get the same text as me?"

"Come get me, Bruiser. Trade me for them. Give him what he wants. Don't let there be more bloodshed, please, just give me over to him."

I close my eyes, clenching the phone in my hand tight enough, I'm surprised I don't break the damn thing. "Not happening, Princess. We'll get them safe."

"And you'll shed more blood. The simplest thing to do is give me over. Let him have me. Save them, and then later you can save me," Gwyneth says softly, her breath hitching. "If you don't come get me, and give me over, I'll go myself. I'll run. I swear I will."

"Don't you dare think about it," I snarl and look at Hammer. "You do that, and I swear when I get my hands on you, you won't walk for a week."

Hammer meets my gaze, and I tell him what she said.

He nods, grimacing. "Hate to say it, but she's got a damn point. Save them, then we save her."

I clench my teeth together, not liking this one bit.

"Brother, we can get her back," Dagger remarks.

"Remember, your woman can take care of herself. She'll protect herself until we can get to her."

"It's not ideal," Malice adds, nodding. "But it would get your sister and the kids out of harm's way."

"Y'all realize you're talking about sacrificing my woman, right?" I sneer, my lip curling in disgust that they would even agree with Gwyneth on this.

"You know I'm right, Bruiser. Save them. I'll do what I have to do to protect myself until you can get to me," Gwyneth utters in my ear.

I let out a harsh breath and grind my teeth. "Fine, but swear to fuck, you get even one damn bruise, woman, and I'm tying you to my bed."

"Come get me." She disconnects, and those words scream in my head.

I'm sacrificing my woman in order to save my sister and her kids.

Fuck. Fuck. Motherfucking fuck.

"I called the number that the text came from while waiting on you," Gwyneth mutters as soon as I pull her in my arms, crushing her to me.

"The fuck did you do that for, Gwyneth," I snap, not letting her go.

"Because I don't want him to keep your sister or

those kids longer than they have to endure this nightmare," she answers, pressing her hands against my chest. "He said that he would be here within an hour to handle the trade."

Fucking hell.

"That fucker is coming here?" Hammer snarls.

Gwyneth twists in my arms and nods. "Yes. That was an hour ago. He said it would ensure that you all wouldn't follow after him. Said there would be eyes on the place to ensure you don't." She pauses, takes a breath, and looks at me once again. "He said that if you follow, he'll have all the women here taken and the kids killed. He hadn't forgotten about Willow, but he's willing to long as I go, and no one comes for me."

"Fuckin' hell," I growl and pull her tight once again. The thought of letting her do this is killing me. "I can't let you go, Princess."

"I don't want you to either, but I refuse to see anyone else harmed in any way," she states sternly and presses her forehead against my chest. "It's the only way, Bruiser."

"I've got an idea," Savage remarks gruffly. "I've mapped out the different ways to get off this property. The potential places the property could be watched from. We got a couple blind spots that even in the dead of night, you can't see anyone going unless they're hacked into Cy's cameras."

"That ain't possible for them to do." Cy grunts. "I change up the coding and security on those cameras daily. Someone would have to be in my room in order to be able to do that. I also checked the wiring last week to make sure I didn't have any issues."

"So, what are you thinking?" I demand.

"Gunner and me take to the blind spot. Get off the property before they get here. We get in place and follow," Savage suggests.

"There's a chance we could get caught following, but it's better than sitting here not knowing what's what or where he's taking her," Gunner states, nodding.

"I still don't like it," I grumble. "I say we stand our fuckin' ground. Get my sister and those kids, then kill 'em all."

"Think, brother, think about them getting caught in the crossfire," Malice mutters.

"I know," I grind out. I can't do that. None of us can.

"It'll be okay, Bruiser," Gwyneth murmurs, tilting her head back in order to meet my gaze. "You do this the way it needs to be done. Then, when you find me again, you'll make them all pay."

"Damn right I will," I snarl, slide my fingers in her hair, grip it tightly, and slam my mouth down on hers.

I kiss her long and deep, not releasing her mouth until the both of us are breathing heavily.

"We'll be okay," she utters breathlessly.

"You're right. We will be, and you better make damn sure you don't get hurt," I tell her, kiss her one more time and let her go. I look at my brothers. "We do this, get my sister and the kids safe, then I'm finding the bastard and killing him . . . slowly."

"Wouldn't have it any other way." Hammer nods, eyes glimmering with fury. "We kill the bastard and send a message of our own at the same time. No one fucks with our club."

"Fuck yeah," Malice states, with a few of my other brothers chiming in with remarks of their own.

The next ten minutes that pass, I spend them holding Gwyneth for as long as I can. Savage and Gunner left out, sticking to the shadows, and reported a few moments ago that they were in place. They also reported they already spotted a couple of Johnathan's men lying in wait.

Gwyneth's phone rings, and she lifts it to show me the number. "He's calling."

"Answer it. Put it on speaker," I tell her.

She does as I tell her and answers. "Hello."

The tremble in her lip and the way her hands start shaking is enough to gut me.

"I shall send the kids in first. Once you're in my sight, I'll let the woman go, and as you get in the car, she can run into the building. None of those men are to step foot outside. They do, and they're dead. Do you understand?" the man's voice on the other end of the line says nonchalantly. It's almost as if he has no fear of this club whatsoever.

"I'll come out alone," Gwyneth murmurs, and I give her a squeeze.

"Good, and you can tell the behemoth if he dares come for you, I will not hesitate in making him regret it," Johnathan remarks.

"He won't come for me." The way she says it so weakly guts me.

There's no way in hell I'm not going after her.

"Then time is ticking, come on out." He hangs up, and Gwyneth drops her head, shoulders shaking ever so slightly.

I take the phone slowly from her hands and tightly pull her in my arms. "I promise you, Princess, I won't let him have you. We get my sister and those kids free and clear, then we get you. Okay? I swear you won't be with him for long."

"I know," she utters as the door opens.

"Unca Ruiser," the oldest of the kids screams.

Hammer intercepts one of them while Malice and the others help with the others. My Prez looks at me, grimaces, and nods. "Gwyneth, swear to all I am, this club will get you back."

"I know, Hammer." She nods and lets out a shaky breath. She tilts her head back and slides her hands up to cup either side of my face. "I'll see you even if it's only in my dreams."

Without giving me a chance to remark, she twists out of my arms and rushes out of the clubhouse. I want nothing more than to run after her. To bring her back here. To tell her what she makes me feel.

Damnit all to hell.

Moments later, my sister comes barreling through the door, tears streaming down her cheeks.

"Oh God, Bruiser," she murmurs, barely making it to me before her legs give out underneath her. "You have to get her back. If you don't, she'll be lost to you. I know what he intends to do to her. He . . . he told me."

"What did he tell you?" I growl, feeling my gut twist even further than it already was.

"He's taking her straight to the airport where a buyer is waiting," she sobs, shaking in my arms. "He killed a woman in my house in front of me and the kids. Said she was of no use to him anymore and that her debt was paid in blood."

"Savage says they're on the road heading east,"

Hammer says, coming toward us, holding the phone to his ear and an arm around the little girl in his arms. He hands her over to Leanna and meets my gaze. "We ridin'?"

"Damn right, we are." There's no way in hell I'm not riding out. I'm not letting this fucker take my woman anywhere. If he's heading toward the airport, there's only one he'd be going to. He wouldn't chance a scene at a large airport. He'd go for the secluded, more private one with the hangers where smaller planes are stored. "Tell 'em he's heading for Grove End Landing Strip."

"You hear that?" Hammer asks, talking to Savage. "Right. We'll be heading out."

I give my sister a squeeze and step away from her. "Go on back to where the rooms are, knock on the doors until one opens. Stay with them until we get back. And give the Gradys a message for me. Tell 'em we got this under control."

"Tell the Gradys you have it under control," she repeats, nodding. Taking the kids with her, she does as I tell her.

I turn my full attention to my brothers. "Now, we get my woman back and kill 'em all."

CHAPTER TWENTY-FOUR

GWYNETH

Fear threatens to choke me. It leaves a vile taste in my mouth, and I swear at any moment I might throw up. Knowing Bruiser will come for me is the only thing keeping me from doing just that.

Sitting across from the man who is now my captor freaks me out. He has a jagged scar that runs along his cheek and forks off to under his ear and along his jawline. His eyes are dark, and he seems so at ease, like he doesn't think anything could or would happen to him.

God, I hope Bruiser is able to get away from the clubhouse and come find me.

"You must have questions as to why this is

happening to you," Johnathan states, stretching his arms along the back of his seat.

"If I did, would you actually answer them?" I ask snarky like. It's probably not the best idea, but if Bruiser doesn't get to me in time, it could be too late.

Johnathan laughs and leans toward me. "I like you," he says, pointing a finger and wagging it. "From the first time I saw you, I knew I'd like you. Too bad to give you up. I have someone of great importance who wanted to buy you upon seeing your picture. Hence, the bounty that was put out on you. I must apologize, though, for your brother. Unfortunately, that was your mother's doing. She claimed it was the only way to make your father pay for his wrongdoings."

"My father's wrongdoings? What, having a mistress? Please, I'm willing to bet she was spreading her legs to anyone who'd give it to her."

"You're right indeed about her," Johnathan confirms and leans back in his seat. "I personally refused to sample her wares, but I know of others who claim she's quite loose, though does wonders with her mouth."

"This I don't need to know," I mutter, crossing my arms and looking out the window at the passing dark scenery.

"You are definitely not like her."

I glance back at Johnathan as he chuckles. "She's

not my biological mother, so how would I be anything like her?"

"This is true. Because she was more interested in her own needs and selfish about every little thing regarding her life, I will inform you that she's where we're going. According to her, she wants to ensure you get what you, as she puts it, deserve."

"Oh goodie, so I get to see Mother Dearest before you hand me over to, what, some sex slaver or something?" I sneer.

"He's not exactly in the business." He grins, showing me his bright pearly whites. I'm willing to bet he gets his teeth bleached. "Who you're going to is a man who runs one of the top cartels I've ever come across. Just think of it this way, you'll get to spend your nights in the beautiful continent of South America. He controls nearly all of Venezuela, and I believe he's got a few homes on various islands. I'm not sure exactly which one he'll take you to."

"And what might his name be?" It's all I can do to keep myself calm. I don't want to think of being sold off. Or given to a man who is a head honcho to some cartel. Or being held captive on some island off the shores of some other country.

"Gabriel Quintero," he answers and straightens himself in his seat. "It was his men who killed your brother to get you out of hiding. He has no problem ordering such a thing. If not for a debt of my own, I wouldn't have agreed to give you to him. However, there's no way I could pass up more money on top of a cleared debt."

I scoff at his nonchalant attitude about the way he's handling all of this. I mean, seriously, he's acting as if it were an everyday occurrence for him.

"Great! So, I get to be given to a man to pay off another debt, who in turn also took me as a payment. Tell me, did you at least get top dollar?" There's no keeping the sarcasm at bay.

"Of course," he grins, nodding, "I wouldn't take anything less."

"Well, good for you." Rolling my eyes, I want nothing more than to make this car wreck and keep them from getting wherever it is they're going to meet this Gabriel Quintero.

The remainder of the car ride is done in silence, and when we turn onto a battered road, I wonder exactly where we're meeting this guy.

"I'm not a stupid man," Johnathan suddenly states darkly. "I knew they would follow, even with men watching. They'd give us enough time to get a head start, but not that much of one. They wouldn't want to take the chance of being too late."

"Where are we going?" I ask.

"I informed the woman I traded you for that we

were heading to the airport to give you to your owner," he answers. They'll probably head to one of the smaller airports. But we're heading to Grove End Landing Strip. It's secluded and only used by private plane owners who are willing to pay for the secrecy. They also know how to keep their mouths shut for a fee."

"Right," I mutter.

This guy is seriously underestimating Bruiser and the rest of the club. He doesn't know Savage and Gunner were out watching. They're close, probably closer than my man is. But still, I know Bruiser is coming. I can feel it in my stomach.

Suddenly, the car jerks and swerves. The driver loses control of the vehicle, and we go off the road, rolling over the edge and down a ravine. The sound of metal crunching screams in my ears. As many accidents I've been to, I've never been in one, not even a fender bender.

Finally, the car comes to a stop, landing upside down. I blink and do my best to assess my injuries. The seatbelt kept me from bouncing around the inside of the car, but the pain in my body is enough to tell me I'm hurt. I reach up to wipe my face, bringing my hand back to find it coated in blood. Okay, so a head injury for sure. Heads bleed, so no big deal.

I blink a couple more times and glance around to

find Johnathan's body lying in a funky position. From the looks of it, his neck is broken. Too easy of a way to die in my opinion.

Outside the ringing in my ears, I can hear yelling and what sounds like gunfire. What the hell?

I shake away the thought and struggle to unbuckle without hurting myself further. I barely complete this task when I hear Bruiser's voice and more gunfire. Or maybe I'm just imagining it's him so the gunfire doesn't freak me out as much as it already is. Slowly, I cross the small space to Johnathan's body, pressing two fingers to his pulse, confirming what I already know. He's dead.

Lovely. Just freaky lovely.

I glance around, fear threatening to make me throw up. I don't do well feeling queasy. I don't like throwing up... ever. I need fresh air. That's what I need. It could help clear my head. Make me less woozy. Seeing the back glass is shattered, I crawl toward it and edge out to the murky sodden ground. How is it that I'm even alive right now?

Regardless, I am, and I need to get out of this ravine before something else can happen to me.

"Ouch," I hiss, cutting my leg on a shard of glass. "I swear Bruiser is going to kick my ass when he finds me. He told me not to get hurt, and here I am," muttering to myself, I scramble to my feet.

I stumble slightly and move closer to a fallen tree to brace myself.

"Okay, Gwyneth, you've got to think. There's no way Bruiser knows I'm down here," I snap and glance upward. I'm going to have to climb up there.

Another gunshot causes me to jolt and a scream to leave my lips. This isn't good.

Wrapping one arm around my ribs, I push away from the tree with my other.

"Bruiser, she's down the ravine, brother. We're trying to get to her, but the fuckers hiding in the trees are keeping us from getting to her," I hear Savage yelling.

"Bruiser," I scream louder than I screamed before.

"Gwyneth," he shouts back. "Hang on, Princess, we're coming for you."

"Like I have anywhere else to go. I don't even know how to get to him," I grumble to myself.

I take a step forward only to slip and fall. My side hits a sharp rock, and I roll forward, unable to contain the pain radiating from everything. I can't even focus on the smell surrounding me. All I keep hearing is the sounds of gunfire and shouting. If this is it for me, at least I know I'm not going out as some cartel leader's sex slave.

I'm sure I should get up, keep moving, try to get to Bruiser, but there's no way I can keep going. It's all I can do to stay conscious. I hate to admit the best thing for me to do right now is wait until the man who holds my heart gets to me. He's on his way, and hopefully he'll be here soon. I haven't heard any more shots fired.

The sound of feet shuffling and rushing through the terrain echoes around me.

"Princess," Bruiser calls out, coming closer.

"Here," I shout, pushing myself up, only to fall back, scrapping myself up even more.

"Hang tight, baby, I'm almost there," he yells, his voice growing closer and closer.

"Gunner reported a jet just took off. Gwyneth's mother was dead on the pavement," Dagger states, and I'm sure he's talking to Bruiser, giving him an update.

In the dark, their forms come into view, and there's no hiding my sigh of relief.

"Jesus, Princess," Bruiser snarls, coming to my side and squatting beside me. "You're one lucky ass woman, you know that?"

"I don't feel so lucky," I grumble and wince.

"I want to know who the hell was on that jet," Hammer snarls, eyes locked on me while Dagger moves to my other side.

"From what I know, it was Gabriel Quintero," I answer for him. "That's what Johnathan had just told me before we ended up going off the road. He's dead, by the way."

"Someone fucked up," Savage remarks. "There was a set of spikes on the road. The driver ran over them. I think whoever put this plan into action wasn't expecting the driver to lose full control. This was a hit. I'm willing to bet it was to get Gwyneth without any money exchanging hands."

"Makes sense," Bruiser agrees.

"Well, I don't care about any of that right now. I just want to get the hell out of here."

"We're gonna get you out, baby," Bruiser says, scooping me into his arms. "Then we're taking you to the hospital."

"No, if Angie, Grady, and Ross are still at the clubhouse, they can patch me up." There's no way in hell I'm going to the hospital.

"Honor can help," Savage adds, agreeing with me before Bruiser can protest.

"Fine, but if they suggest you need further shit than they can handle, your ass is going to the hospital," my man growls, tightening his arms around me.

"That works for me. Just take me back to the clubhouse and away from here. I don't want to have to think about how close I came to being some drug lord's sex slave." Leaning into Bruiser's chest, I allow myself to pass out, not realizing the sizzle in the air coming off the men around me.

CHAPTER TWENTY-FIVE

BRUISER

"I want to get my hands on the fucker," I snarl, pacing the length of the room we hold church in.

Gwyneth was given a sedative not long after we got back to the clubhouse to keep her ass knocked out so Honor, with Angie's help, could work on her. Honor immediately said she needed to be in the hospital, but with her refusal, I didn't want to go against her wishes unless Honor was adamant about it. Thankfully, Savage's woman has connections and was making a call to pull a favor for Gwyneth.

Hammer called church to discuss what all went down tonight.

"The jet Gunner mentioned was logged as being owned by the Quintero family. As we all now know, after what you said Gwyneth said earlier before passing out is, they're a cartel out of Venezuela. Gabriel Quintero, from what I've read, is the head of the group," Cy says and goes further into detail. Mentions drugs and women. They don't deal in guns, though. Which could make what I'm thinking easier.

I stop pacing and look at Cy. "Do you know where that jet was going?"

"From what I gather, it's heading for the Bahamas. He has a villa on one of the islands there. I've been able to hack into some of his stuff so far, and it's where he was planning to take Gwyneth first," he answers, not looking up from his laptop.

"Right." I nod, clenching my teeth, and slide my gaze to Hammer's. "I'm on the next flight to the Bahamas," I announce. "There's no way I'm letting this bastard get another chance at Gwyneth."

"You go, I'm going with you," Dagger states.

"Same here," Axe grunts.

"I'm in as well," Gunner growls. "This shit is getting out of hand."

Hammer slowly gets to his feet and meets the gazes of each of us in the room. He hadn't allowed anyone else in the room who didn't hold rank. This meeting was strictly between those of us who hold a title.

"I know you want to go, but we're going to have to hold off at least for the time being. We need to be smart about this. With the bullshit we went through with the De La Rosas and the Cintron Cartels, we're still at a standstill with them both. We don't need to have the Quinteros on us," Hammer states, furrowing his brow. "I get you wanting to go after them. I'd say go for it, but we got to be smart, brother. With all the shit we're dealing with, we need to deal with it in a way it doesn't blow back on us."

I nod, understanding my Prez. I get what he's saying, and normally I would agree with him.

But this is my woman he was going to take. A malicious grin slides into place as I hold his gaze. "You trust me, Prez?"

"You know I fuckin' do, but I got to admit, I'm starting to question some of the members, and I fuckin' hate that shit." Hammer lets out a harsh breath, plants his hands on the table, and leans forward. "We've got a traitor. I don't know who, but until we do, shit's gonna change."

"Who do you suspect?" Savage asks.

"It could be anyone not in this room," Malice answers, rapping his knuckles on the table.

"We'll figure it out," Gunner states, nodding. "We'll find 'em and make 'em pay. No one crosses this club and gets away with it."

"Until then, whatever we do, we need to do it without that traitor finding out. I'm willing to bet they have some type of connection to Quintero." Hammer looks directly at me as he says this, and I know what he's saying without putting it into words.

"When she wakes up, tell her that I'll be back as soon as I can." Heading toward the door, I grab the doorknob and look back at my brothers. "If everyone goes with me, not only would Quintero expect it, but the traitor could warn them. Me going by myself, you all are here, you can cover me."

"And what happens if you get your ass killed?" Rogue snarls.

"Then my ass was stupid enough to get killed, and we know I'm not a stupid ass." They know this better than anyone. Growing up with a dad like mine, he made sure I knew exactly how to handle myself and that I could do whatever it took to not only protect myself but others around me.

"You better contact us the moment you're in the clear," Hammer orders.

"Will do," I state. "Take care of my woman until I get back. When she wakes, tell her I'm coming back to her." With that, I jerk the door open, step through, and head straight for the doors, my mind on one thing and one thing only.

Six hours later, most of that on a plane, another part of it on a boat taking me to Quintero's island, I finally have sights on the house where Quintero is now inside.

Cy reported to me when Quintero landed, so I know he's in there. He also informed me that Gwyneth was awake and none too pleased with me. Evidently, she tried to leave, to come after me, but they kept her from doing so. Mostly, from what I gathered, they had to knock her ass back out. I also got an update on her injuries. Busted ribs are the main thing, and a concussion. The doc who came by said Gwyneth should be okay but was sticking around to make sure of it. My woman was damn lucky to have survived that crash as it was. Someone was definitely looking out for her, and it kills me she was in that car in the first place. But I needed to save my sister and the kids as well.

Talk about one hell of a guilt trip to save a few, I had to sacrifice the one who holds my heart. It took me all of a second to realize this, and it damn well sucked. Granted, even if I fought against it, Gwyneth would still have been in that car. She'd lay down her life to save people. It's why she's such a good paramedic. It's what she's meant to do.

Just as I'm meant to do what it takes to make sure nothing and no one ever harms her again.

Thankfully, I have my own contacts and was able to get a flight under the radar and the boat I used to get here. I anchored the boat offshore on the other side and swam the rest of the way. I had to wait out the day. There's no way they wouldn't spot me if I didn't. So, I watched from the boat, watching the dock and the movement that I could. Otherwise, I prepared, sharpening my knives and ensuring my gear was all set for when the sun set.

For this, I wasn't using guns. No, this bastard was going to die by my hands 'cause I'm gonna make sure he knows precisely who's killing him and why. I won't allow him to get off as simply as Johnathan did. It pisses me off that the fucker got off so easily with just a broken neck, but I can't change the outcome. It is what it is. What I can do is make sure Gabriel Quintero gets exactly what he deserves.

I don't care if he was just the buyer or not, he was buying my woman, and from what Cy informed me, he was the one behind the bounty on her, not Johnathan. Johnathan was just the middleman.

The moment the sun goes down, I strap up, jump into the water, and swim for shore. It's not a hardship, and I don't mind the workout. The swim helps me focus on what I'm about to do.

Soon enough, I'm walking onto the beach and making my way through the darkness, using the shadows to shield me from view and keeping me out of sight. I come across first one, then another guard, and slit their throats from behind. Neither of them saw me coming.

Moving farther along, edging the property, I climb over the wall surrounding the entirety of the place. I shuffle along, moving for the back doors where, from the blueprints of the place Cy sent me, I just need to get up to the second floor to the master suite.

I come up on two more guards and throw one of my knives in the chest of one while twisting the neck of the other. Both fall into a heap, and I rush toward the back door, check to see if it's unlocked, and inch the door open. Other than a few lights on here and there, the place is quiet and dark.

Good.

I move through the house on silent feet. I don't come across any more of Quintero's men, which doesn't surprise me 'cause not long before the sun set, a boat left with at least fifteen of his guys on it. Probably going to one of the popular islands where bars and pussy are easy to access.

Just outside Gabriel's room, I listen for any movement inside. Hearing nothing but the sounds of moans and grunts, I throw the door open, catching the bastard unprepared as he jerks from the whore he's fucking.

"What's the meaning of this?" Gabriel snaps, his accent thick. "Who are you? How did you get in here?"

"You didn't think you could get away from any repercussions for what you attempted to do last night, did you?" I snarl, stepping closer, drawing a knife from its holder attached to my thigh. "You thought you could buy my woman, have her brother killed, and you wouldn't pay for it?"

"Do you know who I am?" Gabriel questions, getting to his feet. The whore in his bed clutches the sheet to her chest. "I could have you killed for this. Is that puta worth dying for?"

"That woman is my ol' lady. She's worth every damn thing," I answer. "You and most of your men are already dead, Gabriel. If you tell me what I want to know, I'll make your death easy as I did theirs."

"I'll tell you nothing," he spits.

"I was hoping you'd say that," I say, grinning and throwing the knife, hitting my target. That target being his leg. I didn't want him to die quickly, and he won't. That blade I saved just for him. It's coated in a cone snail's venom I'd gotten off one of my contacts. Stuff is deadly. Cone snails are one of the most poisonous sea creatures and worth the money I spent on the vial.

Gabriel stumbles to the bed as the whore scrambles off the bed and out of the room.

"Now, you can either tell me who in my club is helping you, or I can make your pain all the more uncomfortable," I say closing the distance between the two of us. "You're already dying," I inform him and grip the handle of my knife in his leg and yank it out, making him shout in agony. "This blade was coated just for you."

"You can't do this to me," Gabriel grinds out. "I'll make sure you die for this."

I throw my head back and laugh, shaking my head before sobering. "Gabby, buddy, you're the one who will die tonight. You nearly killed my woman with what you pulled with Johnathan. I don't give a shit why you killed the other bitch, but you won't get away with what you did to her. The pain you caused my woman is what you're paying for."

Thrusting the knife in his hand, I twist it, digging farther into the mattress. I leave it planted there and pull another knife from its stealth. "Ready to tell me who the traitor is?"

"I'll tell you nothing." Sweat beads down Gabriel's face, and it has nothing to do with his previous activities.

"Okay." I shrug and press the tip of my knife into his eye socket, not too far, I don't want him to die just yet. I just want to take his sight, well, to dig the eye out in an excoriating way. I do the same to the other while he bucks and tries to fight me away. But the bastard, no matter how much power he holds, is nothing but a puny weasel.

"Ready to talk yet?" I ask once I'm satisfied both eyes are out and dangling. "Or you want more pain?"

"What is it you want to know?" he pants.

"Who do you have in my club that's a traitor?"

"I have no one in your club. It was a debt owed to me by someone associated with the club. They are the ones who did this for me."

So, it wasn't a member of my club. That's good to know. Hammer will be happy to hear this.

"Name?" I demand.

"William Burnts." The name rushes past his lips. I've never heard the name, but I'll get Cy to look into it.

"Appreciate the help, Gabby boy. I've got one more thing to ask. Why Gwyneth?"

"Her mother, real mother, was a beauty. My father wanted her, but she rejected him. The woman who raised her found out I was interested in purchasing her when Johnathan put her picture up for bid. She made a deal with him and then with me. The puta thought she could cross us both and get away with it. Gwyneth would have been mine. A rare beauty who would birth a daughter I could use to seal a deal with the Cintron Cartel."

Well, fuck.

Everything seems to be coming full circle now, isn't it?

Done with the bullshit, I plunge the knife into Gabriel's body stomach and step back. Now, it's time to finish the job.

It sucks that the whore is here, but it'll have to be what it has to be. I'm not taking her with me or helping her escape. For all I know, she'll be in on it with the rest of them.

With quick work, I set everything up I need to blow the place up and make my way outside.

I don't bother sticking to the shadows this time. I stalk out of there and pull out the lighter I found while setting everything in place. I grab some dry grass and light it on fire before dropping it where the flames will lick and spread, moving toward the house.

Turning my back to the flames, I walk away, knowing my job here is done. If he's not already dead, the fire will kill Gabriel and anyone else who doesn't get out of there in time.

By the time I get to the shore, the house is engulfed in flames.

I allow a grin to spread across my lips. No one gets away with harming those who belong to me. I won't back down from killing anyone who gets in my way. They call it a reckoning for a reason, and I'll destroy those who dare come between my woman and me.

Thinking of Gwyneth, it's time to get back to her. She's gonna be pissed, but she'll get over it pretty quickly. I'll make sure she does because damn if I don't love her, and it's time she hears the words.

EPILOGUE

GWYNETH

"I'm going to strangle him," I snap, more than ready to commit murder. It's been three weeks since Simon's death and everything that happened. I do my best not to think about it. It hurts to know my brother is gone. The club has been super supportive and even went to the funeral. It was the first time I'd seen my dad and grandfather, and they seemed to have changed.

I don't know what happened, but my grandfather retired, and my father even took a step back from his company. They're still very much into working, but they both are constantly around. I didn't think it was possible for them to fit themselves back into my life, but somehow, they managed to do so.

Bruiser talked me into letting them back in, and

though it feels weird, I don't mind. I do like seeing them and getting to know both of them. My dad even showed me some pictures of my birth mom and told me a few stories. I look forward to hearing more, though this is all going to be weird for a while. I need to get used to them after cutting them from my life for so long.

"What did he do this time?" Angie asks, looking up from where she's doing inventory on the ambulance.

"He told Cap not to put me on the schedule for another week, and Cap agreed with him." I huff and rake my fingers through my hair. Not working in the past weeks has sucked. I don't like not working. I love my job, and I'm ready to get back to it.

"Maybe there's a reason why?" Mick suggests, shrugging, not looking up.

"What would that possibly be?" I demand, throwing my arms in the air, frustrated by this.

"You'll have to ask him," Angie answers. "Speaking of asking, Rico wants to know if you wouldn't mind if I take on the class until you're ready to come back. Several of the gym members have asked him multiple times when you were starting it back up. I told him I'd talk to you to see if you minded me taking it on."

"You want to do that?" I ask. I miss teaching the self-defense class and working out at Primal, but right now, it's not where I need to be. I need to finish healing mentally before going back. Not that the gym has anything to do with it, but I'm struggling with everything else.

The only thing that keeps me sane is Bruiser.

"Yeah, sure," Angie remarks, nodding, lifting her gaze to me. "It's not like I hadn't been in on it the whole time." Shoving a drawer closed, she grabs her clipboard and hops out just as the bells ring, alerting to a medical call. "That's us. Gotta go. Just another week, and you can be back with us." She grins and squeezes my arm before rushing to hop in the passenger seat while Mick gets behind the wheel.

I let out a sigh, wishing I were going with them, but Cap says one more week.

Unable to do anything else, I stomp out of the station and head for the clubhouse. Bruiser said that's where he was going to be when I left the apartment to come here.

He's in for a rude awakening when I see him. He should know better than to make any decisions regarding me without talking to me first.

The moment I step into the clubhouse, I spot him immediately talking to Dagger and Cy. His gaze connects with mine, and I narrow mine to a glare, seeing the smirk that curls on his lips.

"Hey, Princess," he greets me when I'm close. The big lug wraps an arm around my waist and pulls me deeper into him while tilting his head in my direction with the intent to kiss me.

"Don't you, hey Princess me, you giant ass," I snap and push at his chest. "You talked to Cap about me not going back to work for another week, and I want you to tell me why."

Bruiser grins and tightens his arms around my waist. "Because we've got plans this week. We're going back to the beach and finishing what we started."

I blink at him, and then it hits me. A blush tints my cheeks, and I swear I feel my body start to hum with the need for this man. He hasn't touched me much since that day. What we've done has been sweet, but I want more.

"We are?" The two words come out breathy-like.

"Yeah, baby, we are. I just stopped here to wait on you and talk to these two for a few minutes," he says, gliding a hand up to tangle his fingers in my hair. "Since you're here now, we can hit the road. But first, I've got two questions to ask you."

"What's that?" I stare at him, not sure what he could want to ask me here and now.

"First is, will you be my ol' lady and wear my cut?"

All other thoughts leave my mind completely. I knew what it meant to wear his cut. To be his ol' lady. He'd been saying I was his woman, but him asking me something like this means everything to me.

"Yes," I answer, nodding.

"Second question," he announces. He lets my hair go and steps back, reaching into his pocket while dropping to one knee. "This was my mother's ring, she'd have wanted you to have it. Will you marry me, Gwyneth Rose Haney?"

I don't think I could wish for a better moment or proposal. Biting my lip, I nod and launch myself at him, tackling him to the floor and kissing him.

"I take that as a yes," Dagger barks out, laughing.

I break away from the kiss to meet Bruiser's gaze. "Yes, Bruiser. I'll marry you."

"Good, 'cause there's no way I was letting you escape me. You're mine, woman. The only one for me. Without you, the world as I know it would cease to exist. You're my reckoning, and I wouldn't have it any other way."

Dear Readers,

I hope you enjoyed Bruiser's Reckoning. The next book in this series will be Cy's Destruction. You won't want to miss it to find out who this William Burnts is and what he has to do with the club.

I know it seems so far away, but it will be well worth the wait, I promise you! Until then, there's still plenty to look forward to.

Sincerely,
E.C.

ALSO BY E.C. LAND

<u>Devil's Riot MC</u>

Horse's Bride

Thorn's Revenge

Twister's Survival

Reclaimed (Devil's Riot MC Boxset Bks 1 – 3)

Cleo's Rage

Connors' Devils

Hades Pain

Badger's Claim

Burner's Absolution

Redeemed (Devil's Riot MC Boxset Bks 4 – 6)

K-9's Fight

Revived Boxset (Devil's Riot MC Boxset Bks 7 — 9)

Red's Calm

Brass's Surrender

<u>Devil's Riot MC Originals</u>

Stoney's Property

Owning Victoria

Blaze's Mark

Taming Coyote

Luna's Shadow

Devil's Ride (DRMC Boxset 1 – 5)

Choosing Nerd

Stoney's Gift

Ranger's Fury

Carrying Blaze's Mark

Neo's Strength

Cane's Dominance

Venom's Prize

Protecting Blaze's Mark

Devil's Reign (DRMC Boxset 6 – 10)

Whip's Breath

Viper's Touch

Cyprus's Truth

Devil's Riot MC Southeast

Hammer's Pride

Malice's Soul

Axe's Devotion

Ruin Boxset 1 – 3

Rebelling Rogue

Remaining Gunner's

Savage's Honor

Revenge Boxset 4 – 6

Bruiser's Reckoning

Devil's Riot MC Tennessee

Breaking Storm

Blow's Smoke

Nines's Time

Lucky's Streak

Defiance Boxset 0.5 – 3

Shiner's Light

Devil's Riot MC Mississippi

Fighting Rosemary

Inferno's Clutch MC

Chains' Trust

Breaker's Fuse

Ryder's Rush

Axel's Promise

Fated for Pitch Black

Their Redemption Boxset 1 - 5

Tiny's Hope

Fuse's Hold

Nora's Outrage

Tyres' Wraith

Brielle's Nightmare

Their Salvation Boxset 6 - 10

Pipe's Burn

Faith's Tears

Lyrica's Lasting

Brake's Intent

Speed's Ride

Dark Lullabies

A Demon's Sorrow

A Demon's Bliss

A Demon's Harmony

A Demon's Soul

A Demon's Song

Dark Lullabies Boxset

Royal Bastards MC (Elizabeth City Charter)

Cyclone of Chaos

Spiral into Chaos

Aligned Hearts

Embraced

Entwined

Entangled

Crush Boxset 1-3

Ensnared

Entrapped

Night's Bliss

Finley's Adoration (Co-Write with Elizabeth Knox)

Cedric's Ecstasy

Arwen's Rapture

Christmas Delight

Satan's Keepers MC

Keeping Reaper

Forever Tombstone's

Hellhound's Sacrifice

Outrage Boxset 1 – 3

Mercy's Angel

Facing Daemon

Scythe's Grasp

Mayhem Boxset 4 – 6

Holding Beast

Toxic Warriors MC

Viking

Ice

War

Storm Boxset 1 – 3

Grimm

Maverick

Spiked Raiders MC

Corbin's Conflict

De Luca Crime Family

Frozen Valentine (Prequel)

Frozen Kiss

Heated Caress

Simmering Embrace

Scorched Boxset (1 – 3)

Fiery Affection

Inflamed Touch

Searing Passion

Sons of Norhill Tops

Inheriting Trouble

Dancing Struggles

Burning Tears

Pins and Needles Series

Blood and Agony

Blood and Torment

Blood and Betrayal

Agony Boxset 1 - 3

DeLancy Crime Family

Degrade

Deprave

Detest

Desire Boxset 1 - 3

Deny

Demean

Delusion

Destroy Boxset 4 - 6

Underground Bruisers with Rae B. Lake

Caging Dyer

Finding Reese

Breaking Phoenix

<u>Available on Audible</u>

<u>Reclaimed</u>

<u>Cleo's Rage</u>

<u>Connors' Devils</u>

<u>Hades Pain</u>

<u>Badger's Claim</u>

Sabotage

In a blink of an eye life can be taken, just as it's given.

SABOTAGE

Years ago, I gave up on finding a woman to fit my life. I had everything I needed. My daughter. My club. My bike. Life was good. Then it wasn't.

I came into this life, knowing what I was looking for, but I got lost. When I was able to I traveled the world. Then everything fell apart. My daughter needed me.

Now she's happy and wants the same for me. But the problem is, there's only one woman who catches my eye and she doesn't need to put up with my demons when she's got her own.

Or so I thought.

Thrust into a situation where it's her and me, no one else around, we're stuck together. Together we have to figure this out. If not both our lives are on the line.

Lynch's Match

Once burned the pain is all that's left.

LYNCH

The past is finally come to the present and nothing else can stop the anger building inside me. She was supposed to be my match. The one person who was always mine and mine alone, but that was a lie.

Now she's back in town and I didn't even know it until it was too late. She's going to get herself killed if I don't do something about it first.

With the past always comes the demons and they seem to have targeted her. This is something I won't allow. To protect her, I'll keep her close. Make sure nothing happens to her. Keep the monsters away from her.

However, I have to do this, it won't be easy. She's still my match. The one woman meant for me, but that doesn't mean I have anything to offer her. Nothing more than my protection.

Or does it?

Striker's Yield

Life has a way of making you yield, but it won't stop me from getting what I want most.

STRIKER

The first time I saw her, I knew she was pure. Sweet and shy, it works for her. She's not the type I usually go for, but that didn't stop me from wanting her.

She didn't come around often, so it was easy for me to ignore her. Until I couldn't anymore.

Danger stalks the night and threatens her in a way that draws us in. To protect her, I have to choose, but will I be able to live with it or do I walk?

SOCIAL MEDIA

BE SURE TO FOLLOW OR STALK ME!

Goodreads
Bookbub
DRMC BABES
Instagram
Author Page

Printed in Great Britain
by Amazon